Landmarks

A collection of flash-fictions

*for April Chickadee Bradley
my fine friend and resister,
your words, wit and wisdom
sustain me*
Kia ora e aroha nui
Alex xox

Edited by
Calum Kerr, Angi Holden
and Amy Mackelden

A National Flash-Fiction Day and Gumbo Press publication

First Published 2015 by National Flash-Fiction Day
in association with Gumbo Press

National Flash-Fiction Day
18 Caxton Avenue
Bitterne
Southampton
SO19 5LJ
www.nationalflashfictionday.co.uk

A CIP Catalogue record for this book
is available from the British Library

ISBN 978-1514398081

Dedicated to Terry Pratchett
1948-2015

Geography is just physics slowed down,
with a couple of trees stuck in it.
- The Last Continent (1999)

Contents

National Flash-Fiction Day 2015 Micro-Fiction Competition Winners

Foreword

Putting together an anthology is much like going on a long journey. You start with hope, fear, and wide-eyed expectation. Every turn you take opens up a new vista, a scene you have never even imagined before, a scene being played out just for you.

Yes, it's possible to get awe-fatigue, where you start to take the extraordinary for granted. But then something unique will surprise you, and once more you are riding the wonder-train to Amazeville.

Of course, the catering is probably appalling, and you arrive at your destination tired and sweaty and in need of a stiff drink, but the journey is utterly worth it.

And so it is with *Landmarks*. It has been at times a labour, a journey of miles through constantly changing terrain, but it has never been less than a joy. The stories in here map the geography of everything from the human heart to the heavens above us, and we know you will find something wonderful in here to transport you.

Calum Kerr
Editor
June 2015

In the planning of NFFD 2015 there came a moment when heads were put together, tasked to generate a theme. Someone suggested 'Geography', with a view to encompassing both the literal and the metaphorical. With a topic like that we said, you can go anywhere your imagination takes you.

And you did. We had flash fictions about place and about memories of place; about maps and borders and territories. We had settings which were familiar, foreign or downright strange. You sent us all manner of geography: physical, environmental, human. And all manner of geology: sedimentary layers, ash, sand, rivers, oceans. You sent us fantasy and sci-fi, stories of crime and revenge, lust and romance. You made us laugh. You made us cry.

Our final selection was fought over and negotiated, as are all contested spaces. A settlement was reached, a treaty of sorts. This is it.

This is our map. Or rather, this is your map. These are your Landmarks.

Angi Holden
Editor
June 2015

Hilary Is the Winters of Keith's Discontent

Kevlin Henney

LHR... MUC... MAD... CDG... OKA... PEK... SHA... HKG...

Airport codes poured out of Keith's diary like a tipped bowl of alphabet soup. How he longed for LHR... the overpriced relief of the Heathrow Express... the ranked taxis of Paddington... the enclave of his flat. From Europe to the Far East, from sales to marketing, from clients to suppliers, the newly appointed MD's whirlwind tour was a forced route march intended to impress. Hilary Winters left behind her a trail of star-struck customers, newly motivated middle managers and Keith — body clock blinking, self-esteem in the red.

His goal to impress her with wit and initiative had dissolved into caffeine, melatonin, alcohol and self-doubt.

Wit? His S&M/sales-and-marketing joke had met with her stern correction that it was, "Strictly speaking, an inaccurate portrayal of the BDSM lifestyle." The merest suggestion that Hilary's confidence and control might enjoy a private life fired his jetlagged imagination at all the wrong hours.

Initiative? Arriving in the Munich hotel he'd stammered a few phrases of frown-inducing German before conceding an English defeat. She'd stepped in with fluent German, sharing a joke with the doorman. Keith wouldn't have minded but Hilary then pulled the same trick in Madrid. And Paris. Was it the same joke? Was it at his expense?

Anticipating Okinawa would level the playing field he

discovered "I don't speak Japanese" meant Hilary could apologise in Japanese for not knowing Japanese, before requesting — with appropriate deference and inflection — to continue in English. Beijing brought the revelation she'd studied Mandarin.

Impress? Any mark Keith was leaving was either indelible or invisible. By Shanghai he felt outranked by the bellboy.

But Hong Kong... he had this.

Her Mandarin could stretch to Shanghainese, but not as far south as Cantonese. She'd only ever spent two nights in the city; he'd lived here in his teens. His vocab was rusty, his tones off-key, but he'd been practising, online and off.

The hotel manager approached, smiling. Keith smiled back with confidence and outstretched hand. But as his mouth opened he realised the manager's smile had not responded to him, the manager's eyes did not meet his and the manager's hand...

Was for Hilary. "Ms Winters, a pleasure to see you again. Will you be staying with us for longer this time?" Keith reholstered his hand.

"Mr Lo, the pleasure is all mine. Sadly, my visit is short. Perhaps a drink?"

"Certainly. Let me show you to your room myself. One of my staff will take care of your check-in details and your colleague."

"I've got some things to sort out, so I'm afraid I won't be joining you," Keith said. But the manager and the MD had already found a conversation, a path to the elevator and another reason for Keith to take shelter in his hotel room.

Before the ultimate, double-locked sanctuary of his flat, Keith's diary promised further destinations, his imagination threatened details — repressed in Singapore, tense in Los Angeles, shot through in New York.

SIN... LAX... JFK... LHR.

10

A Secret Weight

KM Elkes

On their kitchen wall is a picture, fading now and the frame wood-grain worn, of Jack and Connie on the steps of Corpus Christi, freshly-wed, both squinting into a summer sun.

Afterwards, they dodged confetti rice hard as hailstones, ducked into her uncle's car, rode silently to the reception, ate sweating sandwiches kept under frayed tea towels, saw good ale froth from warm barrels, clapped at half-drunk speechmakers, danced, talked, nodded, smiled, then left for their first uncertain night of "are you asleep?" and "are you happy?"

In the tepid, whispering morning Connie rose early, took her station at the stove, cooking bacon and eggs. Jack sat at the table, lit a cigarette, drank tea, and when in doubt, smiled. Later there was a walk up the back fields, work the next day and the next and somehow time bowed like the curve of the earth from that day to this, 45 years later.

It is Thursday. Pork chops day. The old saucepan bubbles and Connie sings: "Be Glad That Love Has Come". They have lived in this house all their married life. There has been a decent job away from the factory floor, two children, three grandchildren. It has been a good, steady life.

He still sits at the table as she cooks. And every dinner time, Jack looks up at the picture while he waits.

He remembers so little of that ancient day, feels separated from it, like an ox-bow lake. Except for two things— the secret weight of a bone-handled knife in one wedding jacket pocket, a cutting of rhododendron in the other.

These had been saved from the day before, when he cycled, white knees in khaki shorts, to meet Daisy Brown at the park. She led him into a clearing surrounded by rhododendron bushes, spread her coat and lay down.

"And you getting married! So help me God," she had said, laughing so loud he had to hush her with his mouth and then, at last, it had happened.

"That's it now," he said later, under a sky that echoed with light. For once Daisy said nothing, just lowered her head onto his shoulder.

The pork chops are ready, on the dot. Jack smiles at Connie's thin, weary head as she puts down his plate. They will eat quietly, then she will wash and he will dry and there will be a mug of tea on the sofa and a few "what do you want to watches" and a few "I don't really minds".

And when Connie finally dozes, before it gets too dark, Jack will slip out to the back garden to sit on his bench, wood-grain worn, half-hidden among the dark weight of rhododendron bushes grown from a single, small cutting. And there he will remember, with absolute clarity, a young girl's face and her taste, like a sharp apple, freshly bit.

How Can I Get You to Dance?

Angela Readman

His wife crossed her arms in the kitchen. She wouldn't look at him, not really. Maybe at his boots, flaking forks of dried dirt onto the lino.

'Come on,' he said.

He reached for her hand. It remained firmly tucked. She'd sat still for so long a groove buckled her sandalled foot, pressed against the chair leg. It had to hurt. He wanted to tell a joke, make her laugh. Then, he may have a chance. When people told jokes he felt sort of sorry for them.

'It's going to be sunny tomorrow.'

He looked out the window at strips of red sky like something ripped. She didn't look. If he could get her to see the sparrow on the wall, it would be a start.

It was too quiet. He could hear next door's lounge with its back to him, someone learning violin. Waltzing Matilda. Whenever they jabbed out a wrong note someone laughed, and someone joined in. He turned on the radio to drown them. There was an old song playing, one he knew. He listened for a second in recognition, and dialled the music up loud.

'You remember this?' he asked.

She looked down. He shuffled his feet along to the song, rusty. Hadn't danced in a long time. But in the kitchen, he swayed a little, not perfectly, but still sort of a dance. He didn't see how she could let him dance alone. He waltzed to her, offering his hand.

'Dance with me.' He spun to remind her what dancing is, 'How can I get you to dance?'

If he could make her dance, everything would be fine. He remembered country dancing when he was a kid, stripping off to his underwear to stand opposite a tall girl. He never understood why schools taught it, just for one year, but that year, he learnt how to hold a girl's hand. Learnt to follow her steps, walk in a line, pull her close, and lose her for a time.

There was a space in his head where the girl's name once lived. She had plaits, wore a petticoat, and looked like she may catch something by holding his hand. Yet he swirled her around, let go, whirled her in. She was right there, with him, dancing up a storm that swept away the cold hall, giggling friends, and replaced it with a barn. This is what a superpower must be, he felt. This is mine, I can dance someone into believing we could be somewhere with corn swishing outside, a spread of blue sky. When the dance was over, his partner looked surprised he wasn't lowering a cowboy hat to her, and she wasn't wearing a gown. The barn was just school.

He danced in the kitchen, considering that now, palm stretched, reaching for that one dance. If he could just get his wife to unfold her arms.

Bad Geography

James Coates

I'm behind the fresh fish counter. It's quarter past too early on Wednesday morning. Outside, rain cuts vertical scars from a black sky. My shoes are still wet. The squeaky blue plastic gloves I'm wearing make my palms weep. The fleshy bit between my fingers is itchy; life cannot get worse.

Gary snogged Sadie.

That's all the text said. My phone had beeped at 3am, leaving me wide awake with images of Gary sliding his skilful tongue into Sadie's eager mouth. Bastard; we only broke up on Friday. Bitch; she's had her uneven eyes on him for ages.

From the counter, I select a Plaice and a Sprat. One in each hand, I squeeze their cold faces so their jaws move.

'Oh Gary, you're so sweet.'

'Ooh Sadie...'

'Yah, yah, yah.'

My Supervisor breezes past, so I quickly pretend I'm rearranging the display.

I clock the awkward customer straight away, stomping past the dried pasta and packet sauce section with focussed determination. Rain-washed hair clings to her face like a waxed beard, but I recognise her; Mrs Grayson, my old school Geography teacher. She's clutching an oversized bar of chocolate, held out like it's the Olympic torch and I'm next in the relay.

Why me? Why can't she go to customer services, or Outer flipping Mongolia, or any of the other exotic places she'd constantly informed me I'd never be successful enough to visit.

She slaps the bar onto my counter. 'Is this the same one I've just seen in Superdrugs?'

I reply with open-mouthed incomprehension.

She sighs loudly, then repeats her question with added fury.

I want to tell her I can't possibly know. I want to tell her my feet are cold, my hands are clammy, and that I don't give a dolphin's shiny blow hole if it's the same bar or not.

I want to tell her my slimy Sprat of a checkout manager ex-boyfriend has been snogging my wonky-eyed, cash office slut of a former best friend at a work's party I couldn't attend because I had to be up early to stand amidst a plethora of dead sea creatures while being abused by stupid people, and that she's loopy to be out in this weather looking for chocolate.

Except, maybe I'm the crazy one, standing here in wet shoes with nothing to look forward to except the knowing whispers of my colleagues and the clinging stench of dead fish. Maybe, with her disappointed frowns and D minus markings, she'd been right all along.

From the counter, I select a Mackerel. Facing its beady eyes towards her, I make its mouth move. 'Due to unforeseen copulation, and a tectonic shift in my aspirations, this counter is now closed.'

I flop the Mackerel back into the display, lift the apron over my head and hang it on its peg. Pinging the gloves off, is liberation. As I walk away, Mrs Grayson gapes at me; somehow I resist the urge to squeeze her face.

Colouring In

Shirley Golden

My boyfriend insists on matching motifs: all aspects of the globe tattooed on our bodies: his back and my thigh.

I fear the pain and try to persuade him half each is enough; I joke and say when we're together, the world is complete. But we argue over continents; besides, he fancies the whole for himself and insists we should both be the same.

The outline is tolerable. But the colouring in causes grief; the green, and expanse of blue that creates wave after wave of pain.

I cry but don't pass out.

The tattooist calls me a trooper; my boyfriend calls me a girl, a truth and an insult packed into one. But he holds my hand tight and lets me squeeze as hard as I like. That night, we trace exotic places on the other one's skin.

I work extra shifts at the factory in hope that our dreams might fly.

My pennies never amount to much, and he dips into the jar most afternoons to fund his habits. Only when he passes out on the sofa, do I dare to imagine a new route down my thigh, and I chide myself for being a girl.

Eventually, I cross channel and land mass without him. I make it as far as the sole of the boot and stare across the Ionian Sea; the salt wind lifts my hair to curls.

I feel my leg through layers of cotton and ink, motor memory driving the glide of my touch. For where once dwelt a map, now rests a dragon, her coat a scale of red and black, her tail coiled around my ocean-sized egg.

Sweet Gestures

Chris Stanley

It's an eight hour coach trip from Grimsby to Poole, starting in darkness and arriving at the ferry terminal in time for lunch. They've been on the road for forty minutes and Christian is already so bored he'd rather be at school. He's sitting at the rear of the coach, behind his parents, with half the back seat to himself.

'Try to sleep,' says his mum.

'Can I have my Walkman?' he asks. He clamps the orange foam headphones to his head and tries to get comfortable.

At the other end of the back seat is an old woman with a thin-lipped smile and a Margaret Thatcher handbag. She offers Christian a sweet and he takes a golden lozenge, unwrapping it carefully so his mum doesn't hear. It's creamy and smooth and nothing like the barley sugars and humbugs he's used to. He rolls it against his teeth, happily distracted.

He wonders if the old woman made the sweet. What if she's on her way to Jersey to sell the recipe to the owner of some giant chocolate factory? He chases his imagination into a world where the newspaper headlines celebrate the success of the sweet-making millionaire, wondering if he might be worthy of a mention somewhere in the story that follows.

And then he realises: he didn't say thank you.

It's too late now. There's no way he can thank the old woman without his mum overhearing. But what if she's upset? What if she complains? What did his mum say before they boarded the coach? 'Never speak to strangers.' He's pretty sure this includes taking sweets.

Christian's left leg begins to feel funny and he wonders why the old woman didn't offer a sweet to anyone else. What if they're not really sweets? What if she's tricked him into taking poison and the dull ache in his leg is the first symptom? What if he's dying?

He has to get the sweet out of his mouth. His saliva's taken on a nasty, metallic taste and his tummy feels funny. He searches his trouser pockets for the wrapper, spits out the lozenge and squeezes it into the ashtray on the back of his mum's seat.

There. Done. Seconds later, he's unconscious.

When he wakes up, the bus is stationary. He has pins and needles in his feet but otherwise he's…okay.

'Are we there?' he asks, removing his headphones.

'Just waiting at some traffic lights,' says his mum. 'You slept for a couple of hours. Want one of these?' She hands him a bag of humbugs. 'Make sure you offer them to your friend.' She nods towards the old woman.

'Why?' asks Christian.

'Because she shared her sweets with you.'

She knew! His mum knew! And Christian has no choice but to give away one of his humbugs. He offers them to the old woman and she takes one, sniffing it before popping it in her mouth. Then she winks at him as if to say this isn't over yet.

Countdown

Susan Howe

"Hurry up with that tea," Connie called from the living room. "It's starting now!"

Eric paused in his search and counted to ten.

"I can't find the tea bags."

His wife's tone rose impatiently. "You never look properly. They're in the usual place."

The usual place, wherever that might be. It was anyone's guess these days. Eric's heart thudded to the *Countdown* signature tune as he continued opening cupboards and drawers until he found what he was looking for.

"Quickly, quickly." Connie accepted her tea, pointing to the paper and pen balanced on the arm of Eric's chair.

"What's the rush?" he grumbled. "It's the same every day."

Connie frowned at him over her glasses.

"You know what Doctor Knowle said about exercising your brain. Especially after what happened to your father."

Eric sighed. "He didn't say we had to be slaves to it."

His wife drew a breath, then appeared to think better of arguing as the first letters appeared on the television screen. Eric watched while she scribbled on the pad in her lap, brow furrowed, lips pursed. Her engagement ring flashed against skin altered beyond recognition since the day he'd nervously slipped it onto her finger. With a stab of grief, he realised their game was nearing its conclusion. And yet here they sat every afternoon, watching quizzes, while life happened elsewhere.

Ignoring his wife's cluck of disapproval and the familiar

wave of panic as the *Countdown* clock ticked off the seconds, he pushed himself out of the chair and moved to the window. He eased the blind enough to see across the garden, flooding the room with afternoon sunlight.

"Hey, what are you doing? I can't see the screen!"

Eric turned and gazed at his wife, folded over her notepad, then back outside at a sparrow, dipping and flapping in the birdbath, oblivious to the neighbour's cat waiting patiently below.

"Come on, old thing," he said. "It's a lovely day and we're going out."

Connie dropped her pen and glared at him.

"Whatever's got into you, Eric?" she said. "You know *Eggheads* is on next."

"It'll be on again tomorrow."

"And what about Doctor—"

"I'm sure Doctor Know-all wouldn't mind if we took a day off now and again."

"Well, what about dinner?"

"We'll eat out," Eric said. "By the river, like we used to."

Connie stared down at her hands, not seeming to understand. He took one and lifted it to his lips.

"We should see the world. While we can," he finished, quietly.

She looked up slowly, her eyes strangely bright, and nodded.

He fetched her jacket and she rose obediently, carrying their cups through to the kitchen. Eric glanced at the word she had made – jograffy. Eyebrows raised, he followed her out.

When she was settled in the car, he popped back to check everything was turned off. Retrieving their teacups from the oven, he placed them in the sink, blew his nose, and entered the final round.

Devil's Mountain

Joanna Campbell

Dieter's father stood on top of an apple-crate to see his son's wedding. He blew a kiss. The bride gave the old man a wave through the confetti cloud. Dieter's father pretended to catch a blue horseshoe and a yellow half-moon.

Dieter called out, promising to post some in an envelope. But the secret police opened his father's mail. The paper scraps would flutter out, unseen, to be crushed underfoot.

Dieter watched someone help his father down from the crate and into a Trabant, his face split by the slow sweep of the wipers. The Wall caused mind-sickness, people said. Brains became clagged with wet cement. The breath of peacetime blew, Kalashnikov-cold, on the backs of their necks.

To save concrete, the authorities had filed down Dieter's old home on the border, shortening it from three storeys to one. They blocked the windows and nailed shut the front door. The whole street was felled, blinded and muted to form a section of the Wall. Its shadow darkened the white sheets on Dieter's father's new washing line.

Fate had made Dieter a free man. He was working in the west on the night the division was built.

When he decided to climb the Devil's mountain, his bride went shopping, the confetti long since combed from her hair.

"Why not just forget?" she asked.

But Dieter wanted to look down on Berlin. Not up at bomb-shredded steeples. Not at the Wall slicing through families; a rough blade cutting ragged through bread.

On top of the mountain, its slopes newly studded with greenery, Dieter caught the triumphant scent of grass and blue windflowers. Encircled by forest, he saw his whole city. To the east, the cathedral glittered in the sun. In the west, sun-bleached sails drifted on the river.

But Devil's Mountain was no hummock rising from the gentle earth. It had emerged from the ruptures, cracks and splinters of the past, from remnants of homes and bones; from scattered furniture, torn curtains and smashed sculls.

Deep beneath the war rubble stood a military school so tough the Allies were unable to detonate it. They buried it under the debris instead and called the heap a mountain.

Man-made devastation had created Berlin's new topography, the savagery of the human race now an outwardly natural feature. History had become geography.

From the summit, the city shrank, its landscape distorted. Dieter could be sitting on a wooded cliff, narrowing his eyes at the glare of sun on sea. There might be no Wall growing out of the good earth. No division at all.

Farms were building-blocks with orange plasticine roofs. Cows were tin toys. Dieter's father was not holding a cup of thin cocoa that shook in his hands and diluted as he stared into it.

There should have been a mountain to climb when Dieter was small. He would have held his father's hand, all the way up one side and all the way down the other.

Petty Larceny at the Grocery

Beverly C. Lucey

I don't know what's making me so mean lately. I used to be a nice person. Not volunteer at a soup kitchen nice, or go without buying something online and funnelling the money on over to a site collecting for Needy Somebodies or other. Even if they are kids who need to hop on the smile train. But I'd smile at people a lot. And thank them. And bring something for the hostess of a dinner party every damn time.

Now, I won't even tell that girl in front of me in the parking lot that she's dropped her keys. She won't realize it until she comes back out of the grocery and fondles herself looking for the button on her car starter that opens the trunk. Now, where did she put those keys? Damn.

I've already scooped them up, put them in my purse, and likely will dump them in my condo's big outdoor bin. They aren't of any use to me.

When I saw her drop them I was mostly noticing the boots she was wearing, and just how she rolled her jeans. All confident. She knows the way people are wearing their denim this season, as if she got the bulletin and I didn't. She probably also knows the names of young actors and singers that fill the pages of People and Style. At the dentist I read about Arianna Grande. Singer. Someone named Hozier. Singer. Chris Hemsworth. Actor and Sexiest Man Alive.

All I know is James Franco because he's in everything, on everything, and I saw a pillowcase for sale that had his image on it. Right. There are people who would like to say, "I'm sleeping with James Franco," and wait to make their stupid little joke. I hate them. See? That's mean. Why should that make me cranky? But it does.

I go into the market, buy my usual cooked chicken, a tub of hummus, and out of mysterious spite refuse to buy kale. I hate women who are wandering around with green smoothies and also proudly insisting they are GF people. I hate that it took me two weeks to figure out they meant gluten free. I hate that it takes so long to find crackers that are NOT gluten free for the hummus. I did pick up a bag of frozen spinach that you can microwave in a bag. That cheers me up a bit. People who eat spinach are virtuous by definition.

But I'm not virtuous enough to hand over the keys in the dairy aisle when I pass the girl who has lost them. I do think about it. I feel them in my pocket like a weight. But she's way too involved in choosing yogurt. I hate that. On the other hand, I do smile widely at her as I roll my shopping cart by. I am aiming for the ice cream.

Dinner and Geography

Keith Gillison

The main course arrived. Sandra was relieved for the pause in conversation. A sip of wine, then another one and she began to recover her composure.

Clive had been talking about geography for over an hour now. The science of volcanic eruptions, deforestation in South America and the source of the river Nile had all been covered in exhaustive detail. Breathing in between sentences was a bodily function that appeared to be optional in Clive's case. Sandra's contribution had been confined to smiling and nodding.

In between devouring mouthfuls of shepherd's pie, Clive continued to regale her with further geographical factual titbits. Was she aware of the erosion of the Jurassic coast and its impact on the fragile marine ecosystem of Dorset and Devon? Had she read the fascinating article in Nature about the effect of tectonic plate movement to the topography of South-East Asia? Did she know just how long it takes for sedimentary rock to form? Sandra continued to smile and nod in what she thought were the right places. A waiter arrived to remove their empty plates. He gave Sandra a look of sympathy as he took them away.

'Good heavens, I've been wittering on about geography for ages now. Where are my manners?' said Clive. Sandra smiled. 'A quick visit to the little boys room for me and then I want to hear all about you, my dear.'

Sandra poured herself a large white wine from the bottle

and drank it back in one go. Her head was spinning with statistical analysis of UK average rainfall fluctuations. She'd had some bad dates in the past but this one, well, where to start? Her heart was pounding, her breath shallow. It was the greatest moment of her life. All that expensive therapy and years of denial. There was just no getting away from it – she had a 'thing' for geography teachers. This time would be different though. No more moving house to within the catchment area of her latest obsession. No more criminal charges. No more name changes and no more restraining orders.

She watched as Clive walked awkwardly back to their dining table. The bushy beard, the National Health spectacles, the battered brogues and faded jeans. He was too good to be true. All that was missing was a suede jacket with brown leather elbow patches. Sandra smiled at the thought of Clive wearing one on their wedding night, as he recited capital cities of the world in alphabetical order to her. By an incredible coincidence, she had one that would fit him perfectly in her wardrobe.

Her geography

Rob Walton

Geography saved her. Nothing else would stay in her head. Poems and dates and numbers wouldn't stick, but when Mr Carter mentioned the source of rivers she knew she'd be all right.

Her dad was kind. The garden was big. One weekend her homework was about mountain ranges. They worked tirelessly with spades and shovels. The words became fewer, but something grew.

Human and physical geography were embraced alike. The dining room table was a developing cereal box model of urban decay.

Deserts were easy. Rivers were always going to be hard, but she learned and moved and was taking her dad with her.

He needed something and he knew this wasn't what other dads did, but he would see where it took them.

His dirty finger nails pushed through his hair which he was forever sweeping back until she cut it. When she cut they talked about the other, the absence, and whether making oxbow lakes was appropriate. They knew what others were thinking and didn't care and they knew this wouldn't go on for ever and would never make things whole again. But it made things different and they learned, and days were filled, and nights passed in the deepest of sleeps.

After half term she arrived home at the same time as her dad and saw a mountain planted with delicate winter flowers like wide open crocuses. It looked right and wrong.

They walked around it and looked at each other and again didn't speak and again slept soundly, but with different pictures in their heads.

One day the river became home to a houseboat painted in bright folk art colours and they smiled at the way it bobbed in the breeze and they crouched down to look closely and thought they could see figures through the smudged window, but they merged and counting was difficult and she told her dad not to try and they cleared a skyscraper from the dining room table and ate at one corner.

On the Saturday they did a shop like they used to, and they returned to eat at a dining room table which had been home to warehouses and industrial units when they had left.

They were unsure about their moods and didn't know how to articulate with speech or manual work, so they hugged and wondered, and wondered more.

Then there was a gap of a month and she didn't know where to go, until one day she got involved with words in an English lesson, and they made some sense, and she brought some home and showed them to her dad and they had them in their dreams.

After that things moved quickly and the river was diverted, then filled, and one day the dining room table was cleared and the next day a bowl of their favourite fruit had envelopes propped against it. They opened them, read and smiled, and talked over each other and thought they saw a figure picking flowers on the highest mountain.

Ultima Thule

by Jonathan Pinnock

She teased it out of me when we were lying in bed. Twisting one of my chest hairs around her finger, she said, 'Where do you most want to go to in the world? Somewhere you've never been before?'

I went through the usual list: Machu Picchu, Samarkand, Havana, Pyongyang. Yes, Pyongyang. Why not?

'You forgot Angkor Wat,' she said. 'You always forget Angkor Wat.'

'All right, Angkor Wat, then,' I said, without enthusiasm. She gave me an odd look.

'You're holding back. I think there's somewhere you've never mentioned before.'

I shook my head.

'I'm right, though.' She leaned in and tugged at the hair. I yelped. 'Aren't I?'

She was, of course. 'Thule,' I said eventually.

'I knew it.'

I shrugged. 'But everyone wants to go to Thule, don't they? It's that Ultima Thule thing. A mythical, distant place beyond all borders. Here be dragons.'

'It's not called that any more,' she said. 'It's Qaanaaq now.'

'Even better. Exotic and a palindrome.'

She smiled and bit my earlobe.

I should have known. Three weeks later she announced she'd

got some time off and she was going away for a week. To Qaanaaq.

'Can I come?' I said, trying not to sound too plaintive.

'No,' she said. 'It's too expensive for us both to go. Besides, you're too busy.'

I couldn't fault her logic on either count.

'How will you get there?' I said.

'There's a flight every day from Gatwick.'

'Bollocks.'

'There is too,' she insisted.

'Bring me back something nice to drink, then. And some music. And take lots of pictures.'

'Of course,' she said.

When she came back, she had a tan. She said this was very common in Greenland: midnight sun and all that. But the presents were not what I'd expected. I'd been thinking in terms of vodka or some sort of Inuit pure spirit. Not rum. And the music, while undoubtedly pleasant, had a definite reggae feel to it.

'You haven't been to Greenland at all,' I said as we looked at her photos.

'Have too.'

'That's a picture of a parrot,' I said. 'There aren't any parrots in Greenland.'

'How do you know if you've never been there?'

'Neither have you.'

'Pffft.'

I think it was the palm trees on the beach that did it for me.

'Listen. Are you seriously expecting me to believe you went to Greenland last week?' I said, beginning to feel quite angry.

'Like I'm supposed to believe you didn't snog Mandy Dickinson at the end-of-year disco?'

I gaped at her.

'But that was in 1983,' I said. 'We weren't even going out then.'

'1984 actually.'

I shrugged. 'Yeah, ' I said. 'Fair cop.'

'What was she like?'

'Bit crap if I remember,' I said. 'Liverish.'

This seemed to satisfy her.

'So where did you go?' I said.

'Tobago.'

'Nice?'

'Yeah.'

'Can we go to Thule next year?'

'Can't see why not.'

Have to say I'm quite looking forward to it.

I Am Maps

H Anthony Hildebrand

What?

I am maps.

Which maps?

I am all maps.

Where?

I am all maps everywhere.

When?

I am all maps everywhere ever.

I'm not even kidding LOL. I mean it: cartographically-speaking, I'm the shit.

I am maps. Turn me around. Go on. See? I am spam.

OK...

I am lazing on your dashboard. I am creased in your forgotten cargo pants pocket. I am faded, gum-smeared, smog-breached behind cracked bus shelter plastiglass. I am embedded in your website, scrawled on a napkin, scratched into the sand, pre-plan.

I am x marks the spot. I am pirate booty. (That's what they call me in the clubs, yo.) I am hope, and I am dope, and I am story.

Women can't read me, they say. They lie. Some can't; it's by design. Why? Because I thrill to their touch, their soft fingers tracing my contours, flipping and rotating me, tapping me through their screens, sensually, haptically swelling me, squeezing me, pulling me apart, drilling down into the very heart of me.

Maps like women?

Maps love women.

Men?

It's complicated. Men love maps, but maps... I once said, and you can look it up, it's pretty famous, I said that you can never do anything more deadly than colour in a map. I will kill you! Haha, just kidding. It's semiotics, dudes. You know what I mean.

Any parting thoughts for our readers?

Yes.

When you want me, when you need me: I will take you home.

Keeping in Touch

Amanda Quinn

She sends postcards.

    Sydney
    Hong Kong
    Venice
    Bangkok
    Seattle

'Look at me,' they say, between lines on culture and cuisine. 'See how far I've come.'

London

Tracey Upchurch

Into the city, running with Ali. Sodium rain. Pre-bomb Victoria. Crowd sweating burgers and perfume. Jumping walls to the Birdcage, park lake breeze, night ripples.

Running to the locked gate, climbing, sitting on the bridge, house on the island, who lives there? Exiled queen, hobbit, warden, ghost?

Feet on the bridge, footsteps. Jump the gate running. Dark, dark, light. Covent Garden, jacket potatoes, sitting on coats, pockets picked, leaping down the steps. Crepes in a café, underground. Smoking over Black Russians, selling a friend. She's a virgin, 'onest guv. Shouldn't be funny.

Running to the Empire, getting in for free. Dancing with sweaty men, leaving with Ali. Meeting a pitbull, trying Haagen Daaz. Walking to Clapham, sleeping in shoes. Northern Line to Tooting, swimming in the Lido. Studying on the grass. Smoking the grass. Running. Reading. Running. Feeling. Fucking. Brilliant.

Meeting. Kissing. Leaving. Decorating. Cleaning. Promising, before God. Setting up. Home.

Drinking over dinner, fighting over nothing. Being beaten up, getting ground down.

Crying, stopping crying. Staring.

Remembering. London.

Saddle Stitch

Michelle Keefe

Her finger wears a second skin: a thimble made of yellowed leather, joined with a seam of tiny, black stitches running up and over the tip like ants when her eye-lids droop from sewing too late.

She spares a thought for the cow- and its hide- and imagines its skin hung out in the sun, a flag from a once great country. Her thimble was made from a scrap, no doubt, little more than a postage stamp, left over after the armchairs and coats, briefcases and boots, handbags and shoes, wallets and purses and belts. Now and then, she thinks of her slice when she cuts out pastry for pies.

Her kitchen looks on two fields: dairy cattle in one, horses in the other with girls in jodhpurs, trotting, pony tails swinging, always somewhere to go. The cows plod off for milking and come back empty again.

She writes her Will at the kitchen table and her pen hovers between cremation and burial. Instead she ticks boxes for organ donation with the promise of an after-life for her insides, but what of her skin?

Through the window, a horse returns; the rider dismounts, unbuckles the burnished saddle and heaves it like a throne, still warm.

She signs her Will: The house will go to the children, one day. She leaves her body to science, her skin to the tanner's art.

Blackberries are bursting in the hedgerow. She takes out a rolling pin, and the flour.

North

Michelle Elvy

North is where everything is familiar. There is the wild terrain at the very tip of your island where the Pacific and Tasman meet: Te Rerenga Wairua, the leaping-off place of spirits, with clashing currents and male and female seas Rehua and Whitirea bashing up against each other in noisy overlapping foam. There is the comforting smell and feel of the low beaches of the protected bays where you learnt as a boy to swim, to windsurf, to dig pipis and dive for sweet scallops. There is the memory of your father's hand, a hand that delivered blows across your backside and carved beauty into kauri. A hand that pulled you out of the water after you fell from the skiff one October day off Whangarei Heads and sank down through the deep while the blue got bluer and the light above grew further out of reach. There is a memory of your mother floating away on a warm wind when you were six, all of her flesh and blood and bone turned to dust and released to the sea and sky, sifting through your fingers at the water's edge. You sobbed with sorrow but also relief that she was not part of something called the underworld but airborne now, floating with long white clouds out over the shimmery sea.

North is where you know every turn of State Highway 1 and every dune of the long western beach. North is where you named giant trees that had not yet been named by legend or the Department of Conservation or anyone else: sensible names like Milo and Willy Wonka. North is where you collected frogs and butterflies and snails and geckos. North is where you kissed your first girl but have never seen snow. North is where the call of the morepork, back and forth, *ru ru*, announced the evening like clockwork: melancholic and predictable and soothing.

North is where you reckon you'll return, one day.

But today, you hitch your pack to your shoulder and shake your father's hand and walk across the threshold. You move slowly in predawn shadows. You walk down the path to the edge of the paddock and suddenly recall something else about his rough hand: the feel of it in yours – every day, for a time – on those silent morning walks to school after your mum was gone. Her soft ashes and bone specks caressing your palm, his fingers wrapping tight around yours.

You shut the outer gate and reach the road just as the sun crests over the hill to the east. A familiar autumn wind turns cold: a front sweeping in from the west.

You turn south.

The Owner

Bart Van Goethem

A week after Miranda had moved into her house, she heard a key turn in the lock of the front door. A man stepped into the living room. When he saw Miranda, he looked as stupefied as she did.

What are you doing in my house? he said.

What do you mean, "my house"? she said.

Well, yes, this is my house.

No, Miranda said, I just moved in a week ago.

The man peered at her as if she were a filthy liar.

That's not possible, he said. I moved in here two weeks ago.

Bewildered Miranda stared at the man. She tried hard to collect her thoughts.

Look, you must be mistaken. I bought this house months ago from Mr. Maccaby.

No, I did, the man said.

Just stop this nonsense, okay? I told you I moved in here a week ago, and as far as I can tell, you weren't here.

The man said, Will you believe me when I show you the pictures of the housewarming party I had last Wednesday?

Miranda raised both eyebrows.

The man pulled out his smartphone and showed her the pictures.

But that's my furniture, she said. Those people are sitting on my furniture. How - how is this possible?

The man just gazed at her.

Prove that you took these pictures last Wednesday, Miranda said.

The man showed her the date of the jpegs.

No, no, she said, those pictures, they must be photoshopped, and the date, I'm sure there's software to change the date of a picture.

Listen, the man said, I understand your reaction. I am as unpleasantly surprised as you are. So I would like to suggest this: let's go to the police. Right now, so we can settle this. Okay?

Miranda scrutinized him. He seemed to be a normal man. Not a lunatic.

Okay, she said.

They both left the house. Miranda took her car, he took his. She arrived at the police station before the man. She explained the situation to an officer and then waited. The man never showed up. Eying Miranda, the officer began talking to a few colleagues. When she noticed the doubt in his look, she burst into tears.

***

Did she believe you?

She did. They all do. And I love the glare they give me. They don't believe it is happening and yet, it is. Their truth crumbles, the reality they believe in evaporates right in front of their eyes. It leaves them enraged and powerless. A fine lesson. People are presumptuous. They buy things and call them their own. But they're not buying clothes, a car or a house. They're buying control. The right to exist. Who ever said they could have the right to exist?

No one.

We can't own life. Life owns us.

Uh-huh.

Anyway, are the actors ready?

Yes.

The camera battery is charged?

Yes.

You have the key to the house?

Yes.

Okay. It's 3 am. We have about an hour. Let's go.

Love

Nik Perring

I found Love crouched in the underpass. Her dress was ripped and a dulled red. She was scrawny and pale—she made me think of a waif—and her chin was scratched and her boots were scuffed grey.

I asked her if she was all right.

'Do you need any help there?' I said, and she looked up, a little confused—not quite present—almost as though she'd been drunk the night before, and she gave me a nod. Her eyes were ice blue and clear.

We walked down the street, as the city danced around us in its night, and we found a café. We sat at a table with a Formica top and we drank coffee there, talked. She sipped delicately. The mug made her hands look small.

'And I'm Mike,' I said and I told her what I did. 'Not as interesting as your story,' I joked and she laughed politely and then she asked me why I'd spoken to her. 'Was it pity?' she said. Did I recognise her?

I told her no to both. Said I doubted I'd recognise love if it kicked me in the shin. So she did, under the table, hard with those big boots. It hurt. I could tell that she meant it.

She smiled then and those ice eyes were so clear and I thought that the colour had returned to her cheeks. Her hair fell over her shoulders now, draped around her face, shaping it, and she was so beautiful.

'Another coffee?' I asked.

'You're very kind,' she said with a smile that was as thin as it was whole.

'You're Love,' I told her. 'We've got to be kind to Love.'

She smiled again and her lips were redder now.

'Not just for the sake of it, I hope!' she said, those small hands still wrapped around her mug.

'No. I'd just like to keep you warm,' I told her and that was mostly true.

'Just that?' she said and her eyes were on me and her mouth seemed ready to move into a lovelier shape. It was as though she knew.

'I like it when you smile,' I said, finally, and after a deep breath. And that's when she kicked me again, with those boots, under the table. She was gentler this time. But she still meant it. I could tell.

On Location

Jon Volkmer

Colin Firth shot a scene here, you know. No really, he did. It
was that movie about the British etymologist who runs afoul
of the Mexican insect traffickers. The one with Gwyneth as the
competing scientist slash love interest, and they hate each
other until they have to team up to crack the code that begins
with the mysterious initials U.p. The part they shot here was
that scene where he discovers the chiropractor's office is a
front for the mob's illegal dealing in Aztec bean beetles. You
remember it. They had to close the street down. Barricades at
both ends. The locals were none too happy about that, believe
you me. And then, once the barricades were in place, and all
the traffic detoured, then they had to stage fake traffic
and fake pedestrians to create the image of what the street
would be like on a normal day, i.e., if they hadn't barricaded it.
But they had to do it that way because the real pedestrians can
not be trusted not to turn their heads and stare at the camera,
or to gawk at Colin Firth, or go up to him and say, Mr. Firth
Mr. Firth, can I have your autograph? Not to mention the cell
phones. Don't even get me started. With their iPhones and
what have you. You know there'd be pictures on the
blogosphere— or Firthosphere if you will— before he'd
finished the first take. And it always takes, like, twenty takes to
get it right. A lot of people don't realize that. That would have
given enough time for the Firth faithful to descend on the
street like hordes of Aztec bean beetles. The Firth Fan Club,
the Firth Firsters. It wouldn't take long for them to show up.

And they would only get in the way, with their deucedly debonair unruly dark toupees and their faux aristocratic sweater vests. Anyway. So it turned out a lot of the people who live on this street and would normally be pedestrians and drivers here lined up at the barricade at 5 AM for a casting call where they hoped to be chosen as extras to play people who live on this street and walk and drive on it on a regular busy day. Only they had to promise not to stare at the cameras or approach Mr. Firth or in any way act like they know he's a leading man slash character actor with a certain British kind of standoffish but endearing charm. Hugh Grant with gravitas, as it were. And they had to agree to follow instructions off the nice man with the bullhorn on the stepladder. And they had to turn in their cell phones. Just for the day, of course. They got them back.

Would It Kill You to Smile, Blanca Gomez?

Nuala Ní Chonchúir

We have travelled three thousand miles to be here. And look, these three beauties are our children. If you can't smile for us, at least do it for them. It's really simple with kids: if you are pleasant to them, they like you. What kind of memories of this day do you want them to have?

And do you have to drone like that, Blanca Gomez? Is that dull monotone really the finest you can muster? We'd call it a purr but that would imply something sweetly feline and you are more bulldog than pussy, if you don't mind the comparison too much.

Oh, here come the vows. Might you raise your eyes to us, Blanca Gomez? Might you acknowledge that this is A Big Day? That it means something beyond City Hall paper-pushing; beyond another Green Card, or shotgun, or whatever it is you think we're up to here.

'Rings,' you growl. We misunderstand. 'Rings!' you bark, and we both grimace.

Marcy steps forward and hands them over. She makes goony eyes at us and we try not to giggle. We exchange bands of white gold, squishing them onto fingers inflated by the Manhattan heatwave.

Are you normally stylish, Blanca Gomez, or do you always wear beige accessorised with mushroom and taupe? And is that arms-folded stance your regular ceremonial attitude, or is there

47

something about us that just gets. Your. Goat?

Whatever is going on with you, Blanca Gomez, you can't pop this bubble. Because on this day of May days, we are happy. We are elated and blissed out and content. We have emeralds and peacock feathers; we have red and white roses and baby's breath; we have hold-ups that are falling down and a little too much weight on our hips; we have borrowed pearls and pretty children, an old friend and a sultry sun over our heads. Today we have Avenue of the Strongest, Gobo and all of New York. But more than any of that, we have love. Do you have love, Blanca Gomez? Can you at least tell us if you have that?

Toy Soldier

Pauline Masurel

I find it under the gooseberry bush: a tin soldier that my grandfather gave to you before you could even crawl. You never gave up on playing soldiers. I blame all those Andy McNab books in your teens. And the state of the job market when you left school.

I unearth the toy with my fingers, not realising at first what I've discovered. Its unpainted body is perfectly camouflaged among the roots. I brush away the loose soil and smooth my fingertips over its earth-warmed body.

"Where did you find that?" my mother asked me, the day we brought you home from the hospital. "Under a gooseberry bush," I told her. We both laughed. "I didn't think they made them that way any more," she replied.

But it seems they did. Like they churned out regiments in the Great War. You never got it from me; I was always a home boy, shied away from a fight and happiest at home or digging in a garden.

I turn the toy over in my hands. I want to spit in the dirt and fling it far from me: further than the currant bushes, beyond the rhubarb and over the fence until it's lost on foreign soil. But I can't. I just cradle the inert soldier in my palm. After all these years I finally have a body to bury.

Pen Y Fan

Susan Carey

The air-conditioning cooled Kazia's bare legs as she sat down on the car's backseat.

'Weather hot enough for you?' the driver asked the two young hitchhikers.

Gavin got in the passenger seat beside him. 'Bloody boiling ennit? Nice in here though!'

'Where in Hereford you going?'

'Starting Gate pub. If you can drop us there, that'll be tidy.'

'No probs. Name's Jack.' the driver said.

Niceties done with, Kazia clicked the seatbelt shut and put her rucksack in the footwell. On the empty seat beside her was a khaki beret with a golden emblem of a winged dagger. They took off down the winding road heading out of the Brecon Beacons back towards England.

'On holiday?' Jack asked.

'Yeh, spent the weekend mountain-biking,' Gav said. 'Least I did. Kazia's not one for extreme sports - not outdoor ones anyway.' He winked. 'And yourself, what brings you to these parts?'

'I'm working. Overseeing the Fan Dance for the SAS. I'm semi-retired but they asked me out for this last one.'

'What's the SAS?' Kazia asked as she ran her fingers over the beret's emblem.

'Scuse her, she's not from around here,' Gav said.

'I can see that,' Jack answered. 'Special Air Service. We're the big-shots of the army. Go in where angels fear to tread etc. Who Dares Wins, that's our motto.'

'And you special soldiers like dancing?' Kazia asked.

'The Fan Dance is the last stage of week one in the selection procedure. On Pen Y Fan, the highest mountain in the Brecon Beacons. It's really gone tits-up this time though. Shouldn't tell you, I suppose but it'll be all over the papers tomorrow anyway. Lost one of our lads, didn't we. Only nineteen. Pen Y Fan bloody hotter than Afghanistan right now. No shade and carrying over 25 kilos in this heat done him in. Got heatstroke and it was all over pretty quick.'

'It's a sort of Hunger Games?' Kazia leaned forward.

'You could say that, love.' Jack changed gear to go up another hill.

'Christ,' Gav said.

'That's where I'm off now. Tell the family. I know his dad from way back. We did the Iranian Embassy together. That creates a bond. I know he'll take it on the chin. He's that sort of bloke. You know, old school.'

'But still. Don't envy you, mate. Not one bit.'

Kazia put the SAS beret on at a jaunty angle, smiled into her phone and snapped a selfie.

Gav saw her in the rear-view mirror. 'Have some bloody respect, Kaz!' He reached round and pulled the hat off her head. Her hair staticked around her.

The road flattened as they neared Hereford. Jack pulled up at the Starting Gate pub and Kazia and Gav spilled out into the merciless sunshine.

'Thanks, Jack,' Gav said and shook the old soldier's hand.

Inside the pub, Kazia hooked up to the Wifi and posted her beret photo on Facebook. Straightaway, it got three likes.

Postcards

Mike Scott Thomson

This morning I receive a postcard.

Who sends postcards anymore? It's all Facebook this and Instagram that, these days. Nothing personal about it. Those who take the trouble to buy postcards, handwrite them, stick on stamps, and send them through the mail, must be one of a kind.

I pick up the card. It's an aerial shot of a choppy sea, crashing in white waves against a cluster of ragged islands. A small font says 'Cabo de Hornos'.

There is no message on the other side.

I think: that's strange. I put it on the windowsill and forget about it.

The following month, I get another postcard. This one clearly says where it's from. The entire image is taken up with 'Greetings from Austin', pictures of tall towers and long bridges. But apart from the handwritten address, the rear side is blank again.

This time, I vaguely recognise the spidery handwriting. But I can't quite place it. It goes next to the other card on the windowsill.

The month after, a third one arrives: a beach in Dominica.

Bingo.

A scramble around in my attic later, I find that box of papers I could never throw away.

Our last ever 'Let's Get Quizzical' answer sheet is buried down the bottom. It's lager-stained and curling, but Neil's unmistakable scrawl remains legible.

We insisted he did the writing. He was always the first to know the chemical elements, the Delphic Maxims, the books of the New Testament. He could get the answers down before any of us had a chance to think.

He was usually right.

We usually won.

I'm not sure what happened that last time. Geography must have been his weak point.

The Cape of Good Hope is not further south than Cape Horn.

The state capital of Texas is not Houston.

Roseau is not the capital of St Lucia.

'You either know these things, or you don't,' we told him. 'Don't take it personally.'

'It is personal,' he said, staring blankly into his London Pride.

He didn't show the next week, or the next. Eventually we stopped going.

There was only one question I knew in that round: Camulodunum was the Roman name for which British town?

I don't expect to find him there, of course. But I know what I'll do when I arrive.

The newsagent lifts an eyebrow when I also request a stamp. 'Holiday of a lifetime, is it?' he says. 'May as well send an email.'

'It's for one of a kind,' I say.

We always knew he'd go far. At least we were right about something.

As I put his postcard in a pillar box, I take a look about me.

Ho-hum, I think.

I get in my car and drive back down the A12.

You Promised

Cath Bore

'I'll sing for you,' you promise, but never do. Instead I get excuses and small talk, coy and cute in my ear.

'Sing for me,' I say. 'You said you would.'

You blink and I wonder how your eyelashes manage to get so dark, your lips so dry, ones that peck me goodbye on the jaw, missing my mouth.

I roll on cooling bed sheets, damp flakes of skin sticking to me like static, and take a sly lick of you from my leg. I suck each of my fingers, worming you out from underneath my nails. You are everywhere and I love it, I imagine you singing for me here and now. In my room, you, singing my song, and making it beautiful.

It doesn't work. You're not here. I sniff my arm. Your smell is gone and no crumbs of you garnish my bed. I have nothing of you, so I hum my song, and wish. I close my eyes and follow a ribbon of sound, hold onto it where it pulls me, over mountains and hills, round bends, down steep slopes and up. My calves hurt, stretched then shrinking as I climb, so I stop. I hear it, my song, faint and low. I sway under a navy sky. Night breezes brush my mouth. My lips swell.

I follow my song. I inch up a tree, your bark scratches my inner thighs raw but I shimmy up and up until I peer into a window. It's you. You smile from behind thick glass, impenetrable, opaque, and sing my song, the one I love. You're singing my song, as I asked, but you sing my song for her, and not for me, never me. Still, I settle and listen. It is beautiful, the song and you, exactly as I imagined.

Re: Help

Sandra Kohls

To: ladybird@yipee.com
From: randomboy@whoop.com
Subject: Help!

Dear friend,

I hoping you get this on time. I'm most sorry to bother you, but I'm in terrible pickle right now and urge your assistance. I'm stranded on Kiev, Ukraine and need your help getting back home to Blighty. I was stolen with gunpoint in car park! Can you imagine? It was terrible experience, but looking on sunny side, I wasn't seriously injured and I'm still alive which is most important thing. I was wondering if you could helping me with quick gift of cash and I promise to refund you when I return in two days. All I really need is about 2,550 Euros. Please help!

Simon

To: randomboy@whoop.com
From: ladybird@yipee.com
Subject: Re: Help!

Dear Simon,

Goodness me. That does sound rather annoying! Now, tell me, are you one of my son's friends? I have a dreadful memory these days, but such are the travesties of age. I do remember a Simon who worked with my husband, but that was many years ago. Are you he? You may not know, but John died 6 months ago. It was sudden, of course, but life must go on. That's why I'm inline! Isn't it marvellous? My son set it up for me so I could chat to people and make friends and I must say, I'm enjoying it far more than I thought I would.

Now, tell me more about your adventure. You are lucky! I have always wanted to travel to Eastern Europe. It does sound exciting!

Edna

To: ladybird@yipee.com
From: randomboy@whoop.com
Subject: Re: Re: Help!

Dear Edna

Thank you for your replying. It is utmost important that you sending me money if you can! I have now been arresting and thrown into dark jail cell. I have only bucket for convenience and thin blanket. They say I must to stay here until someone can pay me my fare home. Please help! I know you are kindly and generous woman – John always said this.

I await your reply with anticipation!

Simon

To: randomboy@whoop.com
From ladybird@yipee.com
Subject: Re: Re: Re: Help!

Dear Simon,

Gosh, that does sound rather dull, but I suppose you can't expect the accommodation to be of the same standard as it is over here. How is the food?

How sweet that John used to call me kindly and generous. It is nice to hear these things. As you probably know, John was not a particularly demonstrative man and there were times when I wondered why I had stayed with him for so long. But you see, that's what you did in those days. Not like nowadays where people seem to change partners as often as they change their underwear! I suppose he was like an old sofa; worn and springy, but familiar and cheaper than a replacement. Well, he's dead now, so it all worked out in the end.

I do hope you are still enjoying your travels!

Edna

Spinning The Bottle

Tim Roberts

They all look the same to me: barely wide enough for a car, uncultivated hedgerows blocking the view to either side, and there's horse shit everywhere. So far, the only suggestion of hope on this journey came about 3 miles back. It was in the form of a worn sign claiming that a village lay 2 miles ahead. Since then, all I've driven through has been small, furry and with its innards engrained into the tarmac. This is what happens when you refuse to embrace progress.

I glance at my phone on the passenger seat. NO SIGNAL. Who would want to live out here?

Amy had suggested I bring the satnav. I had agreed and hoped she wouldn't mention it again, knowing my father would boycott it. The old man had an ability to name obscure B roads that was on a par with my knowledge of the current year's tax rules. Of course, I could have paid more attention on the way here instead of subjecting him to my tales of The City. I couldn't even guess at how long the journey to the water had taken us. An hour, maybe? 90 minutes, on the top side?

At a break in the hedgerow I spot something that's not a shade of green. I break hard and crunch the gears to reverse back; the car whines in protest at the mistreatment. I pull up beside a moss ridden, wooden fence and get out. A few cows take a break from grazing to watch me clamber up the fence. Above the treetops, at the far side of the field, the tip of a church spire rises. I release an unsteady breath that I was unaware I had been holding on to. My estimate is that the church is a mile away, but I don't have the luxury of time for a stroll across cattle filled fields. I return to the car and head off down the narrow lane.

A bend ahead bears away from the direction the church was in. I hit the steering wheel hard and curse. A groan comes from the back seat of the car.

At this moment I remember that I've left the fishing tackle back at the lake. I know my father will have something to say about that — he's used that same rod for 25 years. I look into the back where he is lying across the seat. He's still holding his chest but his breathing is a little calmer now.

"I can go back and pick up our stuff later. Don't worry, Dad," I whisper.

I bring the car to a stop at the broken line of a junction; white paint that is a welcome clue to the proximity of civilisation. There are no other signs to indicate which route leads where. My only choice is left or right. I close my eyes tightly for a second, spin the bottle in my mind, and then check the road ahead is clear.

'We Endure'

Cathy Lennon

Row after row of terraced houses line streets of improbable steepness to the top of the hill. Most of the houses are brown, the odd creamy one, sandblasted with pride, shines like a false tooth in a grubby mouth. It's a sunny day but I opt for a taxi. My wheelie case is designed for the gleaming concourses of international travel, not the cobbles and flagstones of a mill town. Listen to me! 'A mill town'.

Six months ago, in a Beijing hotel room, I peered at a smoggy skyline while my mother talked breathlessly of Wright Street. She spat out words like compulsory purchase, care home, disgrace. I was tired. My proud hosts had just returned me from a tour of the Bird's Nest Stadium which had done nothing for my jetlag. While mother ranted, I held up my hand in front of my face and moved it away and back, away and back and thought: 'I am a long way from Wright Street'.

Now with Bollywood music playing, the taxi approaches a new roundabout by the old precinct. In the middle of it the town motto is picked out in wrought iron over a bed of municipal planting: 'We Endure.' Minutes later we turn uphill. A few yards after that, I am seven years old again.

Even when you're expecting it, reality bites, as they say. A line of rubble, five feet high, separates the boarded frontages of one side of the street from the plane of earth that used to be the other. The taxi bounces away and I'm left staring at a house side, diagonally bisected where a stair rail once hung. Upstairs, blue fish swim across a row of tiles, downstairs, a tongue of Anaglypta lolls towards the ground. Beside me a Victorian lamp post leans, skirts of collapsed stone around its ankles.

Silently naming neighbours long gone, even before the demolition, I pace along to where the house had been. I stop and close my eyes. Seven year old me steps over the spotless white step, shouts 'hellooo', runs to the budgie cage, swings on Granddad's chair arm, runs through to the back kitchen, then out into the yard to the coalhouse door. There's a hole in the cement there, that's perfect for flicking marbles into. My fingertips roll warm glass between them.

Flapping polythene in a window across the street brings me back. I stand sifting featureless earth with the toe of my brogues, hand-made in Hong Kong, the trip before last. 'The funeral's at two,' my mother had said. 'St Andrew's and then the Crem.' I look at my watch and then at my hand. I lift it in front of my face and move it away and back, away and back. 'We're going to scatter her ashes there,' mum said. 'So she'll be back in Wright Street where she belongs.'

The view down the valley is different without the houses.

I still know it like the back of my hand.

Coming Back to Primorsk

Anna Nazarova-Evans

This is what we left here in Primorsk, Suburb by the Sea, twenty-eight years ago, following the tank cannons' shadows directing us out of the country, like arrows.

We left brand new white blocks of flats, freshly painted and decorated; the road leading up to the beach busy with people in their cotton shirts and dresses; wise, moustached men selling ripe fruit in more colours than I could name back then, who addressed me as "little girl" and my mother as "beautiful". We left the stalls with caramel almonds, homemade lollies, candy floss and ice cream under pastel parasols to stop them melting in the desert sun; white Volgas, bodywork gleaming as if fresh off the conveyor belt; the fat groomed fishermen cats; and the greatest thing of all – a slice of silver turquoise on the horizon wedged between the flats and wooden dachas like a piece of pineapple in a Pina Colada, smelling of salt and oil and seaweed and all things wonderful, that haunted my dreams for years on, long after we left.

'Don't go back there,' they say when we ask for directions, but Mum is already hailing a cab.

The taxi drops us off outside a rickety hut in the midst of cement dust. The dust blanket covers the road into town, the pavement, the seesaw in the kindergarten. We walk around desolate back streets for a while, until we find that same fork in the road from which we used to be able to see the beach.

The blocks of flats, much smaller than I remember them, have turned muddy and black in places. Rust has stained the sea view balconies. There are no trees of any sort. Four men play dominos on a plastic table by the side of the road, smashing the pieces down hard, their clothes old and grey. One of them has tied his goat to the nearest lamppost and it chews on the remnants of grass by the pavement. Seagulls make sad screeching noises as they fly into the sun. My mouth tastes like cotton wool and I go into a local corner shop to get a drink. The lady behind the counter is wrapped into faded shawls and skirts despite the warm weather.

'Why are you here?' she asks, taking my manats and handing me the change.

'We used to live here,' I say smiling.

'You?' she takes a long measured look at my clothes. I push my Radley bag behind. She slowly follows me and stands in the doorway.

Mum and I try to make out the colours between the dilapidated shapes by the beach, but all we can see is a tall concrete wall.

'Where's the sea gone?' Mum asks shielding her eyes with her hand. We both turn and look at the shopkeeper. She chews on something looking towards the horizon, and for a minute nothing breaks the silence except for the domino players.

'The sea is for the rich now,' she finally says.

On the Beach

Kate Mahony

Down below on the beach, hordes of stick figures gather at the end of the long narrow jetty. Something is happening.

'Look,' I say. 'Look at all the people down on the jetty. There's so many of them, the jetty could plunge into the sea.'

Behind me in the hotel room, you're rifling through your suitcase. You're hungry. You want us to go out even though my feet are tired from walking and every restaurant in Glenelg seems to offer the same fish menu. Something quick, you've said. There's a free bottle of bubbly chilling in the fridge, courtesy of the hotel. You're eager to crack it open. But we need to eat first.

'Yes,' you say. It is your absent-minded voice. You're not paying attention.

From the window on the sixth floor, I watch people walk the white sands in twos and threes, while young ones splash in the waves. On the grass, a Muslim woman wearing a black abaya hands out food to her large family who cluster around her. A gang of little boys play on a big art installation – steel made into huge bronze circles and half circles.

'And look at the sun,' I say now. I have just noticed how big it is. How low it looms over the blue sea.

I think of Honolulu. The year after we were married. A belated honeymoon, due to pressures at work, some financial crisis. We walked all the way to a bar on the waterfront where we could sit with a cocktail and watch the sun set. You had seen the bar mentioned in the guide book. The best place in Honolulu to watch the sun set. It was on the second floor of one of those big luxury hotels that we couldn't afford then.

'Look,' I say again. Because now the sun is dipping, dipping, almost in slow motion.

'Remember how we raced to the bar in Honolulu – to catch the sunset?' The heel of my sandal had twisted and broken, and I had to take my sandals off and run barefoot along the street. 'You told me to hurry, hurry.'

'Yes.' Behind me, I hear shoes being tossed from the suitcase. You are searching for something you've mislaid.

'Live in the moment,' I say suddenly, quoting the words I saw painted on a billboard above a big mall yesterday. But now I add my own, 'For God's sake.'

Then, as I watch, the sun dips down so far it disappears. The sky darkens. The Muslim family packs up; the woman places a small child into its pushchair. The family leaves.

The crowds at the end of the jetty swarm back along it, like refugees fleeing across a border. It is as if everything has fallen silent. A signal has been given. Darkness is falling.

Behind me, I sense you moving. You have come to look out the window. Too late, I want to say. Everything is much too late.

A Curious State of Affairs

Ingrid Jendrzejewski

When Mr. Jackson, our geography teacher, told us that we
were going to have a test on the states, we all expected pretty
much the same thing: you know, blank map of the US criss-
crossed with boundary lines and blanks for us to write in
things like 'Indiana', 'Arkansas' and 'Oregon'.

Most kids spent the week cramming, carrying maps around
like little Bibles, but me, I'm not one for studying, so I did
what I always did and just looked at the map on the home-
room wall for a bit on the morning before the test. I tried to
remember where our state was, and some of the neighbouring
ones, in hopes that Mr. Jackson would, like my parents, be of
the opinion that not much was of importance outside the tri-
county area.

My heart sank when I found out that even Dallas knew
where Rhode Island was and that Madison had practically
made herself sick memorizing the locations of the capital cities,
in case bonus points were on offer. But then, it was even
worse than we feared. When we received our test papers, they
were completely blank but for one line of instruction: "Please
draw a map of the United States, and label each state within". I
could hear groans and shufflings all around, but I could hardly
hold back a grin: this was my kind of test.

I checked the clock and then began to draw. I started with
an outline of the US, as instructed, and then, inside, I began to
draw faces. Fifty of them. I started with the ones I knew about:
Georgia, Montana, Nevada, and Virginia, then Carolina,

Dakota and myself. I added in a few I suspected, like Denver, Tulsa, Charlotte and Helena. I knew about some teachers and added in the most likely lunchladies, then padded things out with a few of the mothers that tended to get around the most. I'm not the best artist in the world, but I labelled each face so that there would be no doubt about who they were meant to be, then titled my map in really large letters, "Mr. Jackson's State of Affairs".

I tell you what, there are easier ways to pass tests than studying, that's for sure.

The Beautiful Game

Sonya Oldwin

I hang around outside the Poplar High Street Tesco's like every evening, keeping half an eye on the use-by-today shelf. I kick a Coke can around to pass the time.

There's a new boy, about my age, who's been here every night this week, too. I've seen him around on the estate, always alone. The other kids say he's a weirdo. But he's got a ball tucked under his arm, Tesco's are taking their time and I'm bored, so I ask him if he wants someone to play with.

'You're a girl.'

'No shit.'

'Girls don't play football.'

'Bollocks, course they do. C'mon, let's play.'

'Potty mouth.'

I roll my eyes and lunge for the ball. He doesn't see it coming.

'Stay put. I'll show ya.'

I run as far back as the entrance to the Chinese shop and kick the ball back. It lands where I wanted it to land. If the boy wasn't staring at me as if he'd just seen an alien, he'd have been able to kick it right back. I run over, collect the ball, return to my spot and do it again. This time, he's better prepared. He kicks the ball back. It bounces away from me. I still control it with my first touch.

'Wow. I've seen Özil do this.'

I grin.

'Arse fan, are ya? My dad says they're for posh gits.'

'No, they're not.'

'I like 'em, anyway.'

We're kicking the ball back and forth as if it's normal. He's not half bad himself and he doesn't mind playing with me, which is all I care about. Even though he's a bit weird.

'I wish I had your ball control.'

'Told ya I'm good, innit.'

'You certainly did. Sorry I said that about girls and football earlier.'

I wonder how a polite boy like him has ended up in my part of town. He speaks proper, and his clothes look like they didn't come from the charity shop. No surprise he's always alone, he sticks out. Kinda like me.

'Crumbs, we're missing the bargains.'

'Crumbs? Why the hell don't ya say crap like normal people?'

'Stop laughing or I won't play with you next time.'

There's no time for bickering and I really want to play with him again. We run inside, rivals like the nights before. But when he grabs the only roasted chicken, I don't fight him for it.

A Face in the Crowd

Calum Kerr

The camera was running, and the station was full. On a weekday it would have been rush-hour, but it was a Saturday so while there were people, there wasn't the same frenetic, desperate, violent atmosphere.

Connor milled amongst the crowd, wondering who was here for him and who was just, well, here. He checked his watch. He needed to get this right. They were counting on him.

His slow meander took him to the centre of the concourse, and he arrived just as the second hand started its final sweep. He stopped in a clear space, put his hands behind his back, and he started to sing.

His light tenor carried the opening notes of the Hallelujah chorus through the hubbub. A few people nearby turned, surprised, and paused to watch him.

Like a slow shock wave, a circle of silence rippled outwards.

Connor kept his eyes forward, but used his peripheral vision to try to spot the others. He thought he recognised a few faces from online chats, but he had never actually met any of them.

He sang alone for the first minute, waiting, counting in his head. And then he relaxed as two voices joined in behind him and two other people emerged from the crowd.

The spectators were forming a ring around them, and more people slipped from the mass, their mouths open, their voices raised, and the mob in the centre grew. Soaring notes reflected from the ceiling and from the tiled walls, and the music filled the space. Connor's anxiety seeped away as he realised it was working.

The choir grew, and grew, as more of the people with whom he had exchanged emails showed themselves to be members of one group rather than another.

But as the mob grew, Connor realised that the audience was shrinking. He rose up on tiptoes to see if people were leaving. But he couldn't see past the thinning crowd of onlookers.

More and more people crossed the line from audience member to participant, and Connor felt a sinking sensation in his stomach.

As the last few audience members smiled, pulled hands from pockets and stepped forward, Connor stopped singing. He turned and waved his hands in the air. "Stop. Stop. STOP!" he shouted, his voice cutting the singing off mid-Hallelu-.

There was a choir of mismatched people standing in front of him, looking bemused. And there was no-one else.

"Is anyone here NOT part of the flash-mob?" he asked.

No-one responded, but the last few people shuffled into their spaces in the assembly.

Connor nodded. He looked around, and nodded again.

He took his camera down from the niche where he had placed it, and turned it off, then he walked away, towards the platforms. Behind him, he heard the hubbub start again, and in his mind's eye he could see the dandelion clock he had built from willing singers, as it was scattered by the wind; unseen, unacknowledged, but perfect for the moment it had existed.

The Gambler

Richard Holt

Nothing more than a sign, a long length of cracked concrete platform and a tin shelter. Only one passenger climbed aboard. Why, in the empty carriage, he headed to the seat opposite me, I couldn't guess. He threw his bag onto the luggage rack and we took up staring out the window as the sun lowered, licking at a horizon of distant peaks.

It must have been boredom that made him speak. You're looking down on your luck, he said.

You could say.

I've ridden a lot of trains to a lot of shit-hole towns. And I've seen plenty like you. No idea where you're heading.

He took a well-thumbed deck from his inside pocket. Pick a card, he said. Before I could respond he added, I don't suppose you're a drinking man.

I took a card from his fanned deck. I do have a little whisky, needs a friend, I said.

If I was to tell you you'd picked out the three of clubs—the exact card I was holding—you might offer me some of that whisky.

I pulled the bottle from my case.

He took a swig then offered it back in return for the card. What you have to understand, he said, is when you're on a losing streak your only choice is to play your way out of it, but there ain't no way to tell how long it will last. How long you been losing? he said.

The last month has been bad.

You're in trouble. He flicked the cards around in an elaborate one hand shuffle. I'll tell you a few things I've learned, he said, reaching for the bottle. Never trust anyone. Ever. Every game is a crooked game. Every deck is stacked. That's the world.

Why you telling me this?

In answer he unfurled a grimy sheet of paper. This here, he said, is what happens when you keep away from doctors so long that when they get their hands on you they hit you with everything they've got.

Shit.

Every game's rigged. I'm holding a pair of twos against a flush. Can't bluff out of a hand like that.

How long you got?

He shrugged. I'm heading north to make my peace, same place as I was born; in a field under the stars. How about another taste of that whisky?

So we hit that whisky hard, lights flashing past us in the black back-country night. And the gambler, he kept talking, like it might be the last time he ever did. Somewhere between nowhere and the morning I fell asleep against the window to the rattle of steel on steel.

I woke in morning half-light and realised the gambler was gone. My bag was missing too. I felt my lapel, in vain, for my father's gold pin—the last thing I'd kept that I could hock. That's when I noticed, on the seat opposite, a poker hand, face up. Five cards—all threes of clubs.

The Next Island

Jamie Hubner

'Can I go play on the beach?' the boy asks.

'Maybe in a bit Jordy,' his father says, swatting at a mosquito on the back of his neck. 'Daddy needs to finish packing.' The father shoves clothes into a holdall. He pulls a leather wallet from his back pocket, ruffles through the Bahts inside and drops it down on the bed.

'When's Mammy coming?'

'Her flight was delayed, Jordy. We're meeting her on the next island.' The father takes the passports and slides them into his shirt pocket, pausing for a second to watch his son unravelling threads from the end of an old rug near the door.

They had shared the hut's single bed. The father hadn't slept. The boy spent the night shuffling and turning. The sweat dripping off his back made them stick together and then peel away from each other when the boy turned, like a child pulling a plaster away from a fresh wound.

As he packs the bag, the father watches the little boy. He often forgets just how little he is. This hadn't been the holiday he had promised him. He'd never been able to make a sandcastle with his own father. The only holiday they had been on, his father drank too much and got into an argument with a family in the neighbouring caravan. He had thrown everything back in the car and driven them home. Everybody's knuckles were white. His own father had a habit of making people's knuckles change colour.

Maybe making a sandcastle was one of those important

things. One of those things that if you miss out on as a child, means something as you grow old. He folds his wallet shut and struggles to stuff it back into his pocket. He walks over to the boy and picks him up from the floor in one arm around the boy's waist.

'We have time for one sandcastle, I suppose.'

The boy smiles and it reminds the father of the way the boy's mother smiles when she gets her own way. He lets the boy down and opens the hut door. The boy vaults down the steps and makes deep footprints in the sand. He sits down a few yards away from the hut and moves sand into a pile with his hands. The father looks along the empty beach at the other huts, shielding his eyes from the sunlight, and then the other way at the empty bar and road. He walks past the boy and turns to face him.

'No good there,' he says to Jordy as he walks backwards, 'you need wet sand.' The boy chases his father down towards the sea. They take handfuls of wet sand and make a pile a couple of yards away from where the waves can lick their feet. The father wonders if children ever really forget their mothers. They use their hands to shape and mould the sand as best as they can without a bucket or spade.

Diverted

Marie Gethins

Life is curved. Backs against concrete, we sit side-by-side: two letter Cs. Our tunnel stays cool in the afternoon heat, dry in the monsoon rains.

Balaraj remembers the time before the tunnels when we lived in a hut. He points to empty mud flats. From our tunnel, I look up at the hill houses with their dark window eyes and imagine being inside one of the squares.

He tells me about big trucks driving down our village road, tyres tall and wide filling the sky with dust. People ran out to watch. The trucks stopped, their dirt cloud turning the crowd into ghosts. Giant metal teeth bit the tunnels, lifted them off the trucks, put the tubes on the ground in a line just like my toes— touching but separate. Then it stacked them three high.

I watch a woman climb to the top row, scramble into the tunnel next to us. 'A honeycomb,' she says and lies down inside. Her feet stick out over the edge, blue sari tumbling like water.

Balaraj is good at finding things in bins. We eat almost every day and have a blanket in our tunnel. Sometimes he finds coloured pens. He writes letters and numbers on the tunnel walls. One day he drew our hut, Ma and our sisters. He showed how the floods came and washed them away, but the heavy tunnels stayed put.

This morning the trucks came back. Men with sticks banged on our tunnels and told us to get out. Women screamed, babies cried. Balaraj grabbed our blanket and helped me climb down to the dirt. Now we stand with the other tunnel people and watch. Machines dig deep into the ground. Metal jaws take our homes and drop them into a long hole. Each tunnel touches the next, end-to-end, making a big grey snake.

Balaraj asks a worker what is happening. 'Flood control,' he says. The man tells us how water from the monsoon rains will go through the tunnels and the ground will stay dry. Soon this place will be as empty as the mud flats. I wrap the blanket around my arm tighter and tighter while I think of Balaraj's pictures, water washing away the hut, Ma and our sisters again.

Double Geography

Jane Cooper

Double Geography was the best bit of the week. Not because I ever learned anything, but because Maisie Phillips sat next to me, and because Mr Davis was the kind of teacher who just droned on and on and never bothered to check if anyone was listening. Sometimes I would watch his rubbery lips moving, surrounded by the sandy beard that reminded me of a hamster clinging to his face, and wonder if anyone had ever listened to a single word he said. His pale blue eyes crouched behind thick -rimmed glasses, never noticing that no-one cared. Meanwhile, I used my eyes as much as I could, to look at Maisie Phillips. She wasn't interested in me, but she let me look at her all the same. Her hair was stripy, like the rocks we had to study on the field trip, and her eyes were the colour of the seas they put in holiday brochures. She made double Geography worthwhile.

As we filed into class on the last day of term, Mr Davis was writing on the board as usual. No-one ever read what he wrote. We sat down, shuffling chairs and books. Joshua Baker got his drawing stuff out—he used double Geography to draw cartoons of the teachers to sell—and Matt Haim settled down for his usual double Geography nap. Other people took out books or phones or make up. Maisie Phillips smelled like jasmine, as she always did, except when she swished her stripy hair, which smelled of coconut.

Mr Davis started talking. No-one paid any attention, as usual. Not until the fire. It was an odd place for a fire to start, in someone's beard. I was looking at Maisie Phillips; I only saw the fire because she was watching Mr Davis and she swore. I liked her even more for that. I looked at him too, then, and watched the fire spread. It looked like a bit of tinsel catching the light at first, before the flames took hold and ignited his whole face. He carried on talking, the pale blue eyes as calm and blank as usual. Then, instead of words, something else began to pour out of his mouth. It was orange and red and so bright that it stung our eyes. It flowed from his open mouth and onto the floor, like fiery vomit, and the room began to get hot. His whole body was alight now, but he showed no sign that he'd noticed. People began to scream and Olivia Jones tried to open the door but it was stuck. We scrambled onto our chairs as the burning lava enveloped the floor and the heat became unbearable.

In those last moments, I wondered what Mr Davis had been talking about all those times that we'd never listened, and I glanced up at the board at the one word he'd written, that no-one had bothered to read.

Run.

Holiday Photograph

Else Fitzgerald

We are wearing matching sunglasses. Behind us, the water is so clear it isn't even blue any more, like gelatine. My hair is wet, which means I've already swum. In the picture, you can't tell that for most of the day we were both grumpy, and we got lost trying to find the right road, and I was sulking in the car. In the picture, you can't tell that by the time we got down to the beach we weren't really speaking. It wasn't even that nice a day really, it was April and the weather was moody and unpredictable, lots of the time it was overcast and kind of cool. But we drove your stepdad's SUV down onto the sand and that was kind of fun and there was no one around because it was April and the weather was crappy. I'd made up my mind to swim anyway, and I could be really stubborn about stuff like that. We stopped grizzling at each other and I got in the water and you mucked about with your camera. I traipsed along the water's edge, picking at seaweed and bits of shell. I took off my bikini top, because I'd never been sort of naked in sort of public before. The sun came out and everything became too bright to look at. We drove along the beach some more. We fucked in the car with the windows down and you tasted like salt and the sand on our skin was uncomfortable but I'd never done it in a car or sort of public before. In the picture, you can't tell that after we drove up off the beach and got lost again trying to find the cabin your aunt used to rent in the summers, and then we fought all the way back to Perth. In the picture, you can't tell that things are already well on the way to being shitty and broken between us. In the picture, the sky is endless and clear and we are smiling and wearing matching sunglasses that hide our eyes.

Forty Seconds

Katie Stevens

The screen blinked almost the second he took his seat and put on his headset. He had to answer in four seconds. He picked up in three.

"Good morning. Thank you for calling Greenvale Customer Support. I'm James, how can I help you?"

"Hello?"

"How can I help?"

"Sanjeet?"

"Mamma?"

"Are you all right? You said "good morning" but it's eleven o'clock at night, and who is James?"

"Mom, I'm at work."

"Mom? Who is this Mom? I do not know a Mom? I am Mamma!"

Sanjeet glanced discreetly around the room, fortunately his manager was not present. The timer showed twenty-three seconds.

"Mamma, I'm supposed to only spend forty seconds on each call. You'll kill my average for the week and I won't get my bonus."

"Forty seconds to talk to my only son."

"I'm not supposed to take personal calls."

"I am your mother."

"My boss won't care about that."

"You never answer my calls, I don't see you any more."

"I'm busy."

"You have no time for your family?"

Sanjeet sighed. He glanced around the room. No one was paying him any attention.

"Look Mamma, I work nights and I'm tired by the time I get home. I need my sleep."

"Of course you do," she replied sympathetically. "Now what are you going to do about Ganesh Chaturthi?"

"Is it that time of year already?"

"You know it is." Sanjeet groaned inside, he had known this would come.

"I don't think I'm going to be able to make it."

There was an unnerving silence. Sanjeet perused the "Avengers 2" poster on the wall opposite as he waited. His stomach turned over with that sick feeling he got whenever he knew he had displeased his mother. There was more to life than Ganesh Chaturthi. A whole other world of things.

His screen began to flash a warning. He needed to end this call or he would be in trouble.

"Could I call you in the morning?" He could have cursed himself for his childlike tone; he was a man, his family relied on his income. She lived in a world where it mattered if her neighbours saw that the tablecloth was frayed, or that her daughter was seen talking to Hafiz whose grandfather was an Untouchable or that her eldest son didn't attend Ganesh Chaturthi. Whilst he lived in a world of 9/11, Enron, Dolly the sheep....

"I don't think there's much point if you're not coming to Ganesh Chaturthi." It was the ice in her voice that changed his mind. It seeped into his gut and filled him with fear.

"I suppose I could ask to change my shift."

"That would be wonderful!" Her warmth returned instantly and the knot in his stomach released. "I'd better let you get back to work."

"Bye Mamma." The phone clicked off. It began to ring instantly. He took a fortifying breath.

"Good morning. Thank you for calling Greenvale Customer Support. I'm James, how can I help you?"

Tunnels

Vicky Newham

I'm plunged into darkness as soon as I drop down the hole. The stench of piss floods my senses and liquid squishes up my leg. My brain clamours to scan my surroundings, to latch onto familiarity and identify threat.

Something touches my hair. Fear clutches at me. I yank back my head and bash it on the side of the tunnel. It's the heat, I tell myself, just a drop of water falling on me. But I've heard their clicks and chattering and know it was a bat.

Then I remember what you said and am spurred into movement: decide which route and keep on the move. If the water doesn't get you, the heat will. Within seconds my eyes are adjusting and I can make out paths: one ahead of me, to the left and right. I slide down onto all fours to avoid the overhang, and, doing what you told me I take the left-hand fork, trying not to think about what's on the floor. Look straight ahead, not up or down.

Damp seeps through the knees of my tracksuit. I'm pleased to be wearing gloves but I'm sliding in sweat. The smell of putrid flesh hits my nostrils and the back of my throat. I retch and swallow, wondering whether it's animal or human. Somewhere, water is gushing. But cut loose from reference points, and with no internal map, the sound is hard to place. If the heat doesn't get you, the water will.

Clunks echo down the tunnels and everything shakes. An earth tremor or overhead train? The last person was crushed in a landslide.

The trick, you said, is to save the head torch. To conserve the battery for a crisis and not risk a sight now which will send the fear into spiral. The rats and the bats, and half-eaten corpses. All around me I hear scratching, feel things brush against my legs and scrabble over my hands. An insect lands on my cheek and flutters into my ear. I panic and scream and shake my head. Lifeline or death trap, I've got to keep moving. If the heat doesn't get me, the fear will.

As seconds become minutes, outlines sharpen and I can distinguish details. But as minutes become hours, everything blurs and I'm feeling dizzy. Look straight ahead, not down or up. I'm following your advice with a clenched jaw. Drained of energy, I worm along the ground. Stones and debris scrape at my thighs and tear my clothes. The tunnel is just wide enough for me to pass and I've hit a bubble of poor air. Death trap or lifeline, a birthing canal. Lost pints in sweat, with nothing to drink nor a rest for hours.

The water's got louder, I feel myself giving in. They've opened the sluice gate, I'm going to die.

But I look straight ahead and see a slither of light.

If the light gets me, the water won't win.

Travels in Ink

Angi Holden

When I was a child I had a globe on my bookshelf. I'd turn it slowly on its axis, picking out the countries I'd visited: Singapore, when my father's work took us abroad; America, staying with grandparents; France, Germany, Ireland on family holidays. I'd touch the places I wanted to visit when I grew up: Australia, India, Egypt.

At university there was a poster on my wall; later there was that office chart Dave liberated when the factory closed.

'They can make us redundant,' he said. 'But they'll not take our dreams.' He bought a pack of brightly coloured pins and pushed them into the soft cork: the backpacked Greece and Italy of student days; the sunburnt Spain of cheap package holidays; our hopes of Africa and Canada.

But then you were on the way. Unplanned, unexpected. We'll still travel, we said. There are baby carriers and travel cots. We were naïve. Unprepared. We had no idea that once you arrived you'd become our epicentre. We had no need to search out the wonders of the world. They had found us.

Naïve, did I say? Unprepared? Nothing compared to that day in the consultant's office, our baby girl playing around our feet, building towers of wooden blocks and laughing as they tumbled to the floor. He tried to be gentle, as gentle as anyone could be delivering such news. I remember little. There was talk of genes and chromosomes, life-limiting conditions, medication and palliative care. Suddenly we were out on the pavement, the sun turning your blonde curls to candyfloss. It wasn't possible.

I look around the small room. Dave is sleeping in the chair by the window. For months he's looked grief-stricken. Now there is a calmness about him, a new peace.

You too are asleep. I trace the outline of a Chinese symbol on your arm, above the cannula that delivers your morphine. Courage, it says. On your shoulder the sun sets behind Everest.

Beneath your collar bone nestle a Thai lotus and a maple leaf; between them a Japanese carp swims lazily though shallow waters. Beneath the cotton blanket are others I can't see, an Australian lizard on your back, Native American feathers on the soft mound of your belly, an Indonesian orchid on your hip. There are ones Dave hasn't seen, like the words *One Day at a Time* inked across one breast. There are ones he doesn't know about; there may be ones I don't know about.

The door opens softly and Claire comes in. She knows them all. You returned from one of your travels brimming with joy. I always knew you would find love. I hadn't imagined it might be with another girl. She is a blessing. She will always carry part of you.

Claire sits on the other side of the bed and takes your hand. She too touches your ink: *Life is a Verb*, it says.

I recall the consultant's words. Life-limiting, he said. He was wrong.

Useless Without The Other Half

Vanessa Savage

We were fitted together at the wedding, two tectonic plates bonded together, soldered right down the middle by the registrar; a seam that was smooth but undulating, a map of our lives, each bump and twist a memory, a piece of history that made our coupling unique. No one else fitted together in the same way.

That bump – our first loss; a lump made of grief that lives permanently in our chests. That curve in the seam is a smile – the goats: Remember? We tied them up in the garden, but they got out and I had to chase them down the street in my dressing gown, you laughing so hard you couldn't stand up. In the early days we lay awake at night staring at each other through the darkness, whispering secrets and dreams that got woven into the seam.

The end began with a spot of black growing deep inside you, a tremor, barely registering on the Richter scale. Then it spread out, rusting a hole right through, eating you up, blood-red rusting edges flaking away, growing and growing until there was nothing left but the seam that held us together. Not shiny and new anymore, but faded like an old scar, part of us. We held onto that, you and I; a lifetime, a lifeline in that meandering seam. (Remember the beach – that caravan we had? Remember our daughter, the first time we held her?) But the rust wouldn't let go. It gobbled up every last bit of you, sucking the life from your bones.

And now there's just me, the broken half of a once

beautiful machine. They tried fitting another half to the raw seam, but I could still hear your voice whispering through the gaps, the seal was never going to be strong enough. I tried to numb the torn edges – with drink, with gardening, with a hundred hobbies started and abandoned.

But the edges won't heal, won't scab over. They just bleed.

I did try at first. I got up in the mornings and I washed and I ate. But then I'd sit at the table and think what now? And the longer your chair remains empty, the less the distractions work. So now sometimes I forget to eat, can't be bothered to wash.

Now I've stopped trying they've left me here, an island adrift, one more piece of junk in a box full of it. No longer really living, I wait on standby for the rust to bloom on me.

Occasionally, someone comes along, picks me up; blows the dust off. "What about this one? He's in good condition, lots of life left in this one."

But then someone else will touch the jagged seam, hiss as a sharp edge draws blood, and pull away their hand. "No, he's no good – chuck him back. He's useless without the other half."

Wall Map

Emeline Morin

Maria knows where she wants to go.

Every day she studies the map on her wall, carefully adding pins whenever she thinks of a new place to visit.

Sitting on the edge of her bed, she looks up at the wall, admiring her morning's work. A small constellation of coloured dots.

Dan never wants her to put the pins up. It ruins the wall he says. We'll have to re-plaster it he says. Why should she care for the wall? She wishes the wall wasn't there. Nor all those stupid rules. She wants to run away, escape this house and its dull inhabitants. But they won't let her.

So when they're not looking, she goes through all the drawers of the house to find new pins and hides them in her pockets. They can never take all of them from her.

She then spends hours daydreaming, pinning down the countries and places where she will go as soon as she leaves.

The jungles of South America. Iceland. The pyramids. St Petersburg.

Just as she thinks of a new place, Dan opens the door and walks in, without knocking.

He looks up the wall, sighs, and yells:

"Angela! Can you come here, please?"

Maria hears Angela's hurried footsteps in the corridor.

"Yes sir?"

"What did I tell you about letting Mrs Russ have the pins?"

"It calms her down sir," she pauses and looks at Maria, "otherwise she tries to run away."

He sighs, "What is she even doing putting holes in the wallpaper?!"

Maria grunts and turns towards the window. She hates it when people talk about her as if she was not there.

"I think, sir…I think she believes it's a map."

"A map. Right."

He looks at Maria and seems to hesitate a second, he points at the wall, "Mrs Russ, this is a blank wall. There is no map. No map."

Maria ignores him and looks away. Dan turns towards Angela. "Take them all off. Immediately. You hear me?!"

He walks off and Angela starts taking the pins off one by one, standing on the only chair in the room. Maria remains still.

When she is finished, Angela sits next to her "Mrs Russ… Maria…Don't tell Mr. Dan ok?" and leaves a handful of pins on the bedside table before walking away.

Maria looks up at the map, empty, and full of promises.

Welcome to All Souls' Park

Gemma Govier

Please choose an appropriate route from the map below: Route A for the adventurous (including the tree top trapeze), Route B for the anxious (avoiding the trapeze) and Route C for the suicidal (avoiding the lake). Please DO take a red balloon from the stand to your right if you feel the need.

Scooters and bicycles are recommended for the steep, slippery section marked to the west. Those who get up enough pace can freewheel almost to bionic speed and skid just before the large oak tree at the end of the section. Please DO stay close to the edge of the bank as any falls can lead to down the hill roly-polies or even crunchy leaf-rolling in the autumn.

You will find abundant wildlife in the park including many squirrels. Please chase them as they greatly enjoy it and they particularly appreciate playing peek-a-boo round the many oak and beech trees to the south. Feeding is permitted and rainbow sweets may be purchased in our café for this purpose. DO NOT ignore them as this can cause offence.

In the spring, please DO make pink rain by shaking the magnolia trees hard. Mermaid hair can then be created from the fallen petals. In the autumn, brown rain can be made in the same manner with any deciduous tree and goblin hair created with the fallen leaves.

Playground equipment is provided for the use of all age groups from newborn to adult. Please DO play trolls and billy goats from the top of the climbing frame with any patrons passing underneath. This helps to satisfy requests we receive for squeals from the adjacent All Souls' Nursing Home. Newborns using the tunnel slide should be tickled at the top and bottom to enhance giggling.

Refreshments may be purchased in our café and all beverages include free spiral straws. Please DO use these to blow bubble-mountains as you then become eligible to enter our bubble-mountain competition for your age category. Octogenarians are currently leading on this, so we encourage septuagenarians to blow harder.

Thank you for your attention, please DO let go of your balloon and make a wish on your way out.

The Psychiatrist's Shoe

Nod Ghosh

There's a shoe under the patio at Mum's house on Flower Street.

I know, coz I put it there.

I did it the year after me Dad died, so I guess I was like nine or something.

Mum sent me to see Clive Silver coz I wouldn't talk to nobody. She'd tried all the cures she could think of, like making me wear an iron key on a red string, or trying to smack the words out of me. Nothing worked.

It wasn't like I was dense or owt. I was pretty good at me lessons. I could write faster than anyone in me class, and I knew how to draw an internal combustion engine.

Doctor Silver never forced me to say nothing. But he always told Mum to leave the room. One time he put a spoon in my mouth, and had a look at the inside. Another time, he did all these drawings and asked me what they were. They looked like maps of the world. Well I'll be damned if I knew what they were when he didn't even bloody know. I didn't say nowt.

It were on the third or fourth visit, when he was checking what happened inside me pants when I coughed that I thought, you're just a dirty bastard. I ran out of there with the filthy pervert's brogue in me hand. God alone knows why he'd taken his shoes off to examine me on that squeaky leather couch.

I ran back to Flower Street as fast as I could. We were

having a new patio laid. Mum were gettin' it done with the life insurance money. There were all these pavers standing against the wall, and the workmen had stopped for a fag.

I dropped Clive Silver's shoe into the foundations they'd dug, spat on it for good measure, and then shoved some earth over it.

By the time Mum came home, the patio were finished.

"I ain't never fuckin' goin back to that Silver fellow again," I told her.

Mum smacked me for cussin'.

But what the hell, at least I was cured.

Who Can Hear The Screaming?

Kirsten Anne McKenzie

If your home is so far removed from those of your neighbours, does that make the screams any less loud?

Lorna pondered this from the security of her feather eiderdown as she pulled it tighter around her ears. The screaming down the hall, as incessant as the summer chorus of crickets, pummelled her ears.

Perhaps this time a sister would be born. A sister who'd skid through the miles of panelled halls with her; hide in the over-grown gardens with her; a sister to share delightful secrets with her. A brother would be useless. Or would this new baby go the same way as the last one? Straight to the angel-strewn graveyard behind the big house? A plot of bramble-strewn land so far removed from the house, that in winter she almost forgot it was there.

Lorna had several friends there she'd visit in summer, when she was allowed. Quiet friends those marble friends, and in winter she missed them more than she could say.

The screaming woman down the hall was not her friend. She was merely the deliveryman, the courier if you like. The person who was meant to provide her with a sister. Lorna normally gave her no thought, except on nights like these, where the woman's agonised screams annoyingly interrupted her dreams. Dreams of neighbours over the fence. Of school - a hop, skip and a jump down the road. Of a family toasting marshmallows with ruddy cheeks in winter, children all jumbled up together, woollen scarves tangled with Labrador puppies and gangly limbs.

She was sure in the morning a sister would be waiting for her. If only the screaming would stop. She'd do anything to stop the screaming.

The sun barely had the strength to rise in the wintery countryside. Lorna woke, eyes puffy from lack of sleep. With electric excitement she flew out of bed, her feet hardly registering the icy temperature of the wooden floorboards. She flung herself down the silent hall, the long empty hall, past dozens of doors, all shut to her, till she reached the door at the end.

Solid wood. Painted stark white. A dull brass handle high up. There was a time when this handle would have reflected the girl's face, there was also a time when she had been unable to reach the handle, it was so high up. But not now. No, now she was tall enough to turn the handle all by herself, without using a stool.

The door silently swung open onto a room as barren as the countryside, apart from the man in the coat by the window.

"You know you're not allowed out of your room until you're collected Lorna," he uttered quietly, resignation all over his face.

"The baby? Did she have a girl?"

"There is no baby. For the hundredth time, they're dead, and have been for twenty-three years. Since you killed them."

"But the screaming?"

"Just in your dreams Lorna. Just in your dreams."

The Blue House

Cath Barton

From above it looked like any other house in any other town. Like one of the fifteen that had been built on the acre of orchard of our childhood. Like one of the three hundred which were, even now, going up on the field where, as teenagers, we had done all the illicit things. Where in future there would be no grass in which to tumble, no thickets in which to hide. Because, everywhere, They were watching.

It looked normal, the blue house. From above, viewed on the computer screen. But it was clear that it was not like other houses. It wasn't the colour. That was a quirk, but a permitted one. A harmless anomaly, which doubtless amused Them. No, looked at from road-level, there was a real anomaly. I clicked around. Double-checked. Normal arrangement of windows, standard conservatory on the back, tiny garden, narrow parking space. On all four sides everything was as I expected. Except the front door. It was open. Who would dare to leave their door open, so that They could step inside? So that even the casual internet viewer, like me, could step inside? Which I did.

There was a hallway, like any other hallway. In the permitted colours, the two tones of grey. I walked through, on the screen. The door to the left-hand room was closed, but I clicked on my mouse and walked in. Virtually. I prodded the easy chairs. Virtually. They would be comfortable, in reality. There was a table in an exotic wood, six chairs around it. Very austere, very proper. The walls were, again, in the permitted colours. It was normal. However. When I turned round to leave the room I found that I could not do so. There was no longer a door.

I told myself that this was not possible. I was a virtual visitor to the blue house. The solution was simple. Log out. But I found that I could not do so. In front of me there was a beckoning. I was obliged to follow. The room now opened out. It no longer had enough corners to be what it was supposed to be.

I found myself back in the orchard. I was permitted to walk through the orchard of our childhood, the blessed acre. There were apples on the trees. I almost laughed. How crass of Them, to try and recreate the garden of Eden. Surely They did not think I would fall for that one? I did not actually laugh. But something made me turn, virtually, in time to see the blue house fading. Then it was gone.

I spoke sternly to myself. Enough of this nonsense, I said to myself. I took another deep breath, switched the computer off and, with a little cry of triumph, turned round and jumped out of my chair. But the room had changed. There were not enough corners. There was no door. There was another beckoning, and this time it was not virtual.

Saharan Shades

Santino Prinzi

I

Back and forth, I rock on the camel. They said it wouldn't hurt. Darkness surrounds – I place my faith in the guides. I hold on, the camp is near, with it a promise of fire and food. I want to walk, I tell them I want to walk, but they make me stay on the camel; snakes, they warn. Mine hurts.

II

A blaze centred in a ring of wooden blocks. Constructions that are half-tent, half-hut about twenty paces from the centre envelop the seats. I imagine looking down and seeing a fiery eyeball staring back at me.

But this isn't fierce. It's a welcome. Others are here already – they've been cooking for us. Open arms, open doors (I hope nothing has crawled inside my tent-hut), and they gesture for us to take a seat. Our rucksacks hit the sand and we sit and wait. They bring plates full of tagine and chanting as others bang drums and shake tambourines.

The air is full of warming joy.

III

Night: I never thought the desert could be cold.

IV

Outside. Scraping. Pattering. Bounding. Sniffing.

Inside. Heavy-breathing. Imagination. Sweating. Watching.

Outside – they're there – whatever they are – hungry – searching.

Inside. My mind rages almost as wild as whatever beast is on the other side of my door. I can hear them. I can faintly smell them – can they smell me? I listen. No-one else is awake; their sleep is undisturbed by nightmares. They're still sniffing, scrapping around searching for food, but they're getting quieter. My eyes start to feel heavy again.

V

It's morning and there are others, like me, standing still and watching the distant dunes. The creeping sun is the only other sign of life.

It's coming; a glowing emergence from the line that breaks the horizon. Through my sunglasses I watch it move, and then I remember that it really is the Earth under me turning, rotating – face the sun, swallow the stars.

I watch the light begin to conquer the darkest places.

It bursts.

VI

Out of the corner of my eye I can see you on all fours watching us from afar. Your pack have left you for now. Everything is motionless except you and I. You're unbecoming, or is it me? We are the only disturbance here.

Landmarks

Ian Shine

I painted the roads yellow, orange or pink and wrote their names and numbers along them, then began dragging canvases embroidered with green oaks over the local forest. I daubed dark black outlines around important buildings and pumped paint into the rivers and lakes, to make them print-quality blue. I stitched dashes of bright-green astroturf into the ground to mark out local footpaths, then circled our town and laid out ropes behind me numbered 40, 50, 60, 70. Finally, I set up lasers at regular intervals on the edge of town to divide it into squares, then called her and said it was safe to go out.

She had her map marked with her house and mine, and when she looked around she saw the page brought to life in front of her. I talked her through the first part, and it was going well. "See, you can read a map," I said, and she cried with joy. But then the sky started crying too, and its tears leaked onto her map. The ink ran and the paper began to rip, and as she yelled into her phone I told her to stay calm and tell me what she could see. She said there was a foaming river and a rainbow road, that some buildings were bleeding oil and she couldn't move because her feet were caught up in ropes. I told her to move towards a laser, but when she got there it shot her in the eye and she yelled that she couldn't see.

Thankfully her tag was still working and she came up on my GPS. I found her unconscious under one of my dripping oak canvases, her wavy hair running off her head like a waterfall. I traced my finger along the contours of her face, and her make-up ran off on my fingers. When I got her home I stripped her naked and found all the tattoos. I placed my hands on where it said chest and pumped once a second. After 30 seconds, I did what the next tattoo said and breathed into the part marked "mouth" while holding the part marked "nose".

I carried on until the ambulance came, but it didn't make it in time. "Some idiot's covered the roads in paint," the driver said. "It's a mess out there."

They eventually took her away and told me she wouldn't be coming back. I followed her progress for the next few days on my GPS, until her little dot vanished when they put her in the ground. That night, because it was a case of emergency, I did what the box she'd made told me and broke glass. In it there was a map with the roads coloured grey, the rivers brown, and the contour lines all tippexed over and wax crayoned green. I took it outside and started walking towards a place she'd marked with an X.

Third Shadow

Tim Stevenson

My daylight self is waiting for the train, counting the minutes as my shadow stretches across the platform, mingling with all the others, holding their hands; it has no wrinkles to give away its age, suffers no thundering of the pulse when climbing the stairs. There is no pain in its chest.

I haven't told anyone, and I call that secret my second shadow. The place within that hides unspoken words amongst the unlit, votive candles, the place my mother and my friends can't see.

The train is late, so together we turn and stare back along the tracks, waiting for the engine and its inevitable, unstoppable cargo. I move closer to the edge.

Once my shadow was smaller, younger, reaching for my hand against the wall, playing my games in reverse. It was invisible to my mother's eye and her worries about dirt and every schoolyard rash. How I envied it.

Now there is another, a third, the one inside me, already misshapen. Revealed by science, shot through with X-rays, it's different from the other two.

This one is alive.

But, unlike my lifelong companion, my third shadow knows nothing of the warmth of sunlight, or the simple joys of playing with trains.

But it will.

Fingers Crossed

SJI Holliday

The husband is all neatly pressed jeans and tightly folded arms; he sneers at the collection of old framed paintings. The horsey wife flicks smooth hair and reveals expensive earrings.

'Look at this, darling,' she says. He scowls and mutters something under his breath.

The dealer takes his cue. 'Hello,' he says. 'Have I seen you here before?'

The woman turns. 'Oh no,' she says. 'We're not from the area, in fact we've never—'

'We're on our way to Southwold, actually,' the husband says. 'Beautiful place.'

She throws him a look. 'We saw the sign for the antiques centre off the A12. Thought we'd stop by.' She smiles. 'I love this painting,' she says. 'Is it old?'

'Ah,' the dealer says. 'Not that old. Early seventies actually. You know Ronnie's work?'

She cocks her head and wrinkles her nose. She looks like one of those little dogs that people carry in their oversized handbags. 'Ronnie?' she says.

The dealer lifts the painting carefully off the wall. 'Kray, of course. He painted at Broadmoor...'

'Ooh, did he?'

The dealer nods. 'He was huge fan of abstract expressionism. He was inspired by Pollock, of course. This is an original.'

She looks over at her husband, raises one eyebrow.

He sighs. 'We'll have it,' he says, pulling his wallet out of his back pocket.

'Don't you want to know how much it is?' the dealer asks.

The woman smirks. 'Money's not a problem.'

The dealer nods, wraps the painting in brown paper. 'It's valued at five, but I can do it for four-fifty, cash...'

'Fine,' the husband says. 'Can we get out of this place now? It's making me feel grubby.' He throws the money on the counter and strides out of the shop. She shrugs and trails out behind him, gripping the painting tight.

She'll be straight on the phone to her friends when she gets in the car, the dealer thinks. He can hear her now 'You'll never guess what we've just bought...'

The dealer folds the pile of notes in half and slides it into his back pocket. He smiles to himself as he closes and locks the door. He walks through to the back shop where a young boy in spattered overalls is sitting at an easel, flicking red paint at a canvas already covered with black swirls. He looks up at the dealer expectantly.

'Sold?' he says.

The dealer nods. Bends down and ruffles his hair. 'Nice one, son. Do us another one, yeah? There'll be another couple of mugs in here in a minute. Fingers crossed.'

Disputed Zone

Barbara Leahy

'It is a question of geography,' the man with the gun says. 'When you fell, you crossed the border.'

'I saw no border on the map.'

'Your map does not recognise our borders.'

His English is slow and emphatic; an educated man in frayed fatigues.

A scarf is bound tightly above his forehead. He points in the direction of the gully where they found me and I see that he lacks two fingers on one hand. The other men, or boys, squat around him. They used a machete to cut me down. One of them holds it balanced on the tip of its blade and he swaps the handle from one hand to the other, his eyes never leaving my face. Another spits something brown and foul towards my feet.

'I'm with a group of climbers,' I say. 'They'll be searching for me.'

In the glare of the sun, my head pounds, and I long for the cool of the rock crevice where I hung for a day, maybe longer.

The man with the gun smiles an unlovely smile of stained teeth. 'No one is searching for you,' he says.

I was overwrought when they found me, I could have told them anything.

They are agile climbers, lean and muscular. I hung from the rope, giddy at being rescued until I felt their boots in my back.

'I'm a climber, not a soldier, not a journalist. I can be of no use to you.' He laughs at this, and the others join him in a low rumble of mirthless laughter.

'We make use of everything we find,' he says. He unslings the gun from his shoulder, hands it to one of the men. From a rucksack he takes a small device, a camera perhaps, and a sack.

'It is nothing personal,' he says. 'Merely a question of geography.'

Fable

Oli Morriss

She wasn't sure how long she'd been alone for, but it had been a long time. In fact, it might have been forever. She couldn't remember a time when she wasn't so isolated, and she certainly couldn't remember the man with the antlers. He was a shadow.

Being alone didn't bother her. In fact she welcomed it. Other people always seemed so busy, and animals were so dirty. There was too much movement and noise and mess when there were things other than herself to be concerned about. She was neat, and she was quiet, and she almost never surprised herself.

She closed her eyes and wandered through empty streets of an early evening, the orange sun leaving stripes in the parched ground between buildings that were as much made of shadow as cast within it. She couldn't remember seeing the man with the antlers again, but did remember seeing a bird as it shot past her ear and into a broken window in the side of one of the buildings. She stood still for a while, staring at the window, hoping and terrified that she had imagined it. If the flash of colour were to reappear, it would confirm and deny her suspicions. Eventually, as the saturation drained from the edges of her vision, she opened her eyes and returned to the room. She shouldn't have gone out.

That night she dreamed of the bird and didn't dream of the man with antlers. The bird fluttered through her mind and she reached out a hand to it, but it darted just beyond her reach every time. The next morning when she awoke she sat in a corner until the bird disappeared.

She spent the day looking for the bird without leaving the room. Apart from a bed, the room was bare, but there was a window which she left open as she searched, just in case, but she didn't see the bird, or the man with the antlers. She couldn't understand why it had been there and why she had seen it and why she wasn't alone any more. She didn't like not being alone, so she kept searching to try and find nothing.

As she ducked beneath the bed again, she leant off balance and her hand scratched along the wall, drawing blood from her knuckles. She uttered a cry of surprise and staggered upright into the window, smashing it. She was breathing heavily. She hated surprising herself. The bird flew between the jagged shards of falling glass, its wing beats distorted with the light and causing myriad rainbows to spin across the walls and ceiling. She looked at it, unblinking, and raised her hand.

The bird fluttered into her palm, its wings beating the rhythm of the room and reflecting her heart's own metre. She ran her thumb across its head, feeling its soft feathers and delicate frame beneath her hand. It was so fragile.

With a jerk of her fingers, she broke its neck.

Love in Different Time Zones

Jane Roberts

The art of sending a parcel is a lost art, for sure. The true calling of one, who has loved. The packaging should be correct in terms of its postage stamps, so that the receiver should not be embarrassed in any pecuniary way. And the wrapping should not only be sturdy – to withstand any turbulence in transit – but should also give nothing away. No hint at all of the contents within. For where would be the finesse, the gloriousness of the surprise?

Maurice, he sent parcels. First and foremost though, he was Maurice the Traveller, not Maurice the Sender of Parcels. It was a joke between my friends – "Your husband is a Morris Traveller – just like the car!" Except he was Maurice, all French and sleek – a sports car, not a chugging, quaint wardrobe on wheels. Yes, this sports car of a Frenchman used to zoom about so far and wide across the globe; only then, came the parcels – all sent home to France, to me, in the 6th arondissement, Paris, the City of Love.

*

The art of selecting precisely the right contents of a parcel – a present only to be imagined in one's wildest dreams – is a fine art indeed. Only one who understands a lover will comprehend such an art.

The collection from Maurice's travels: a crystal bowl from

Austria; antique Jade from China; a kimono from Japan; a rare orchid from Colombia; an ancient scroll from India...

All those far-off places where all those other women reside. All those gifts I never wanted, surrounding me in our bohemian apartment. So I know exactly what to send those women – the ones with whom he spent all of his time.

*

The accompanying note should be brief, explanatory, and courteous. It will need an unemotional, careful, calligraphic hand.

"Dear (fill in space),

Maurice is dead. Please find enclosed."

A signature is not always necessary.

*

Post Scriptum

The act of posting a parcel is a joyful one, an act of letting go. There is no art involved unless I count the artifice of shrugging to the post office clerk when she asks if my packages contain noxious items. There is a list of toxic substances, which do not pertain to my parcels; their contents far too special to be thought commonplace illegal.

"It really does cost an arm and a leg to send a parcel abroad these days, doesn't it?" says the post office clerk.

"For someone, it does," I answer.

I'm sure Maurice couldn't agree more, as I imagine his mistresses opening their parcels with delight, their smiles cascading into their necks as they remove from exquisite packaging...a hand, a head, an arm, a leg...

A Place in Time

Ruth Doris

I sit on the high stool, dangling feet groping for the foot rest. An old man wearing a tweed coat and a flat cap comes out past me through the swing doors, trailing the low drone of pub chatter in his wake.

This is the first time I've been back since. This time I'm alone, propping up the counter with a literary-looking novel and a pint while the barman bustle around; twisting, turning, pouring, batting banter to and fro. Their dance is hypnotic. I'm thirsty, but wait, loath to disturb the creamy head settling atop the black.

As I sit and watch and drink the light ekes out of the day and drinkers in twos and threes and more barge in through the wood-polished doors bringing with them the cigarette-scented air from the street.

For a long time this place existed as a shadowy backdrop to my life. Old wood, stale beer, worn upholstered couches, the rise of a winged eyebrow in response to a two-fingered salute, tall tales lubricated by beer and whiskey and god knows what else.

Time and alcohol were consumed here at a faster pace than in the outside world. Inside was a noisy stillness, blanket-safe, edges rounded. I looked forward to winter then, the blistering, blustering of the city set off against the window-glow, intimate acquaintances, its talk and its merry little songs rationed carefully until the green hope of spring arrived.

I shift and slide off the stool, touching the tip of my shoes to the floor, reach for the strap of my handbag.

I give a quick sweep of the room, the snug beyond, the counter, the punters oblivious.

I won't be back here again. The spell has been broken. Time is a place. And that place is over.

Five Travellers in a Small Ford

James Norcliffe

Five travellers in a small Ford travelled across the Ardennes. The Hautes Fagnes. The High Fens.

The fifth traveller, strapped in a car seat, cried with hunger.

Clumps of cotton grass rose from the bog land on either side.

The car pulled off the road for the fourth traveller to nurse the fifth traveller.

The sky was grey and despite the late spring there were patches of snow in the shadows.

The third traveller puzzled at his mobile as the navigation system was awry. Luckily, a signpost directed the travellers towards Eupen.

The second traveller, seated beside the third traveller, regretted not making muffins or packing fruit, as like the fifth traveller, the other travellers were hungry.

In 1940 Eupen was declared Judenfrei. Its citizens celebrated.

The first traveller sat in the shadows of a deserted stadium and put his notebook to one side.

He was a liar.

There was no fifth traveller, no fourth traveller, no third traveller and no second traveller.

This was okay. For this is fiction.

In 1940 there were no Jews in Eupen.

This was not okay.

This was not fiction.

Scattered

(After Mike Blow's Aeolus' Cabinet)
Emily Koch

Eva thought she was safe inside.

In the exhibition hall, Tommy dragged her from table to table, the heels of his new trainers flashing red as they hit the tiled floor. His little fingers clung too tightly to her left hand, making her gold wedding band bite into her skin.

Eva looked over her shoulder through the sash window at the horse chestnuts outside, leaves trembling in the March breeze. She was safe inside. The windows were closed; the wind was shut out.

Tommy tugged on her hand and Eva looked down.

'What?'

'Look at this one, Mummy. What is it?'

He pointed at an oak chest with twelve small drawers. It was on a table alongside a laminated sign reading: Aeolus' Cabinet. Interactive artwork. Pull open the drawers and see what you hear.

'How could I possibly see what I hear?' Eva muttered.

Each drawer had a label. Tommy pulled on the handle of the one marked Cierzo, Spain.

A gushing howl tumbled out of the open drawer. A bitter, bullish gale.

Eva froze. She thought she might be sick.

'Close it!' she snapped.

'But –'

She reached a hand out and slammed it shut. She thought

119

she was safe here, away from the haunting sound of the wind: a constant reminder of Ralph's ashes. Why had she so foolishly released them into mid-air, over the cliffs on the Yealm estuary? If she had scattered her husband in the bluebell woods overlooking the river, he would have melted into the land and stayed there. He wouldn't be ghosting her, like he was now - fluttering on the breeze.

Inside, she should have been protected from the wind. But now this—this—what was it?

She stared at the chest of drawers and leaned in, her heart still racing from the shock of the sound. She re-read the label out loud. 'A cabinet containing winds collected from around the world.'

'Why did you close it?' Tommy whined.

Eva's mouth opened, closed. How did one explain to a four-year-old?

'How do they catch them?' he asked.

'What?'

'With a net?'

'Maybe.'

Eva looked at the labels. Košava, Serbia. Puelche, Chile. Which one carried Ralph? Her panic subsided as she read the names. Was he on the Santa Ana winds, over California? With the brown pelicans, flying north from Mexico? Or on the African Harmattan, whistling over deserts and dunes?

Slowly, letting go of Tommy's hand, she opened Mistral, Chinook, Bayamo. One by one. When the sound escaped, she leaned in and pursed her lips, parted them, and dropped a breath into each one in turn, before pushing the drawer closed.

She heard Tommy explain to a stranger behind her. 'It's okay. She's just kissing the wind.'

The Somewhere Road

[36° 55' S, 174° 27' E]

Alex Reece Abbott

Hacked into ochre cliffs of crumbling clay, the West Coast road is all hair-pins and switchbacks, graced with a treacherous scattering of loose metal. Along the cliff-edge, jack -knife gashes cut into the scraggy ti-tree offer a succinct testament to nature's cruel bias; the narrow serpentine route is more than most drivers can handle.

Mrs Nelson can't remember why she exists anymore but she moves on, steady and calm, a woman on a mission, her driftwood staff bleached as an old femur. Her wrinkled face is burnished brown as a pecan shell; her hair, day dress and slippers whitened with gravel dust accumulated on her journey. If she can remember the world's superficial, cosmetic values and the make-over fussing of the bored nursing-home carers that she's left behind, then she clearly doesn't miss them.

In the hot, sweet lupin air, jet black pods crack and pop like corn. She pauses on the verge and unknots the handkerchief that serves as her head-scarf. The wind pummels her with gritty blasts, driving wafts of sharp iodine from the kelp-strewn shore. Drifts of sand haze her view as the purple-black dunes are swept into a huge glinting canvas of wind-etched patterns.

Buffeted by the boisterous wind, her driftwood stick falls to her feet. The next gust snatches the handkerchief from her vein-corded hand. It floats above her for a moment like a white linen cloud. Lured by the siren song of gulls and gannets, she follows it with another step forward and a smile.

How the Earth Began

Jenny Woodhouse

He yawned, so powerfully that everything around him would have shaken, if there had been anything capable of shaking. But in all the vast empyrean there was nothing but light, song, and the gentle breeze of millions of beating wings. Angels, archangels, cherubim, seraphim, all with no thought but to praise him. Nothing else. No shade, no sky, no land, no sea, no up, no down. He wanted more. He wanted hardness and roughness, contrast, conflict.

He raised a finger and a small cherub floated to him. It did its best to bow, bracing its feet against a small cirrus cloud which offered it no purchase. That was the problem. He needed solidity. He craved solid ground. He would even welcome a good hard brick wall to bang his head against.

'Call Lucifer!' he commanded.

In a moment, just a few aeons of eternity, his favourite angel was before him.

'I need conflict. I need variety,' he said. 'I don't want to have dominion over a chocolate box. I need opposition. I need an enemy.'

'Are you asking me to rebel?' said Lucifer. 'Me, your most faithful servant? The one who loves you best?'

'Yes. You're the only one I can trust to do it properly. So I want you to rebel. Fall! I want you to be damned! Go hence into darkness.'

'With respect, Almighty, I don't see how I can. There is no darkness. No shade, no up, no down. Nowhere to stand firm, nowhere to marshal my army.'

'Easily done,' said the Almighty, who was, after all, omnipotent. 'You shall have your battlefield. Let there be land, sea, sky, let there be horizons.'

He pointed to a cloud, rounded it with a pair of golden compasses, laid a pattern of blue, brown, and green on its surface, and set it spinning.

'Let there be Earth!'

Your Body Is Terrain They Can Map Now (Not That That Helps You, Much)

Amy Mackelden

The Registrar shows me the layers on an already dated monitor, pointing at white spots like chicken pox marring otherwise perfect slides. Says, "You know what this is? Has somebody told you?" Last night Google gave me more than I wanted, like a date declaring love only eight days in. Please.

I didn't want to believe it, the internet search engine vomit, a scaremongering symptom list tabloid of Kardashian misappropriations. The Registrar asks if I want kids, which seems soon. I guess my physiology catalogued onscreen in front of him, explicit as Tinder or Match, is compatibility mulch. Plus, medications make birth defects, see. So he's either into me or it's his job to read side effects out. Coin toss.

"I'm ordering all the tests," he says. "In the MRI, don't move this time." But I didn't; bodies just do what they want when nerve endings strip. You can't control a thing, when you think about it.

They map my brain again in March, like a force-watch of George Clooney films I shouldn't see once. I forget my CD; the owner of the Millennium mix which sticks in the machine is long dead, as I wish to be, while Robbie Williams' Angels plays on a loop. Did I slow dance to this with a person, like, ever? Or just that Michael Jackson one, while Alex kissed Jo down the hall?

I am East

Sarah Hilary

Back to back in duffle coats, we sit, optimistic notepads on our knees. Facing away from one another, pointing our attention in all directions. We are four—a compass. I am East.

North and South are a torrid affair, never speaking more than two words with their mouths, but South's hand shakes when he brushes North's corpulent thigh and a swell of tea slops in the lid of his glass-lined flask. He has given the cup to North, whose lips are pressed to its rim.

West keeps his own counsel, worrying about his aged mother back home; I ache with empathy. A scrub of hair sprouts from his stony chin like lichen.

We are studying the stars. We have equipment, a box with batteries, and wires. South calls it our UFO detector. He pronounces it, 'You Foe'.

Beneath my feet—the thrum and rhythm of the earth, this planet's bloodless pulse, an obstinate push of plants and grass, the fractious chiming of fiery plates at its expiring core. It creeps into me, a kissing chill I cannot quantify. I concentrate, retrieve my focus—retract, reduce, exist only in this moment, this infinitesimal configuration. The scratch of North's teeth against the worn plastic rim of the cup, insect-tick-ticking of a watch at West's wrist. There are complexities here that I am only just beginning to grasp. I need more time, to study them more closely.

North and South tremble, the needle swinging between poles, a torturous metronome of attraction, repulsion. Magnetism. West is a mess, excreting salt at neck and groin, a soft tumour as yet unknown beats in his gut with a life that is already death and—

A blunt pressure fills my chest, as if a muscle-mass is gorging there, its ventricles gluing to me, superior vena cava, inferior vena cava—my own internal compass.

'There!' North points skywards and we scribble coordinates, frantic in our failure.

Three pairs of eyes return to the sky.

I watch them watching.

I need more time.

National Flash-Fiction Day 2015 Micro-Fiction Competition Winners:

First Place

Fly
Rob Walton

I'm rushing to push my lunch box in to my bag when I see these two who must be flying a kite on the green triangle outside the school because she's holding a length of string, showing him how to thread it through his fingers, but then I realise she's teaching fly fishing with no river for miles and the nearest polluted anyway and I look again, and she's reading him Ted Hughes and he's hanging on every word as he casts better than anyone I've ever seen, and we all realise that rivers are just a bonus extra.

Second Place

I want someone who wants me so much they don't care about grammar

Laura Tansley

On a canker of a concrete wall in a ground-up grey car park the colour of chewed gum a lover paints in lower case 'your nicer than my wife' above the butt bumper of a blue Fiesta. Each morning it waggles its way out of the space like a preening duck presenting. And when the bay is empty I lie on the earth to feel the heat of tires, the smoked breath of exhaust fumes and high-humidity whispers.

THIRD PLACE

A Weekend Away
Diane Simmons

When I struggled off the train, you laughed, 'You've brought rather a lot.'

In formal hall, I copied how others ate, tried not to grimace at the musty wine. At the theatre, you laughed when an actor spat into the audience. I tried to look like I thought it funny.

I tried to enjoy the beer you bought me in Trinity College bar, tried to like your boisterous friends, was pleased when one asked, 'What are you reading?'

I didn't understand why everyone laughed when I replied, 'The new Ian Rankin.'

But when you laughed, I understood you.

HIGHLY COMMENDED

Marks and Sparks

Ian Shine

Her online dating profile said she was into M&S, so I proposed we meet up at our local shopping centre. I've been helping her with her dyslexia for a few months now, and she's been giving me the time of my life.

The Pacifist

Nick Triplow

Old man Wilson, he calls himself a pacifist. Exchanges opinions and anecdotes for drinks at Danny's Bar: a cut price raconteur preaching non-violence. Last night I discovered he carried a loaded .38 in the pocket of his reefer. I said, 'How d'you square it, this turn the other cheek shit, with the thirty-eight?'

He boot-heeled his cigarette, gave a smile that showed gaps where teeth used to be. 'Wouldn't feel right bein' a pacifist without it.'

"But—'

He pulled it, cocked it and rested the business end against my forehead. 'See son, how peaceful that makes you feel?'

A History of Ants in the Sugar Bowl

Julie Sawyer

"Little blighters are back again" Stan said. "Look" he added, finger stabbing the sugar bowl. Margo looked. "This'll teach 'em" Stan muttered, pouring boiling water from the kettle into the frosted glass, grunting with satisfaction as a dozen or so agonised black forms caught mid-syrup. Margo imagined she could hear their tiny screams. "You'll have to ant powder the place again" she said. Stan glared at the offending bowl and harrumphed, before stomping out to the shed. Touching the recently emptied matchbox in her pocket, Margo watched him go; knowing that she now had a whole afternoon to herself.

And A Bottle of Rum

Garreth Wilcock

"Then the Pirate Queen sliced my ribs with her cutlass and I fell to the deck as she left."

He lifted his gown to show the gruesome scar to his niece.

"So how did you get off your ship and into Papworth Hospital?"

"Glad you asked. Mermaids towed my ship to shore, and my parrot stole a mobile and called 999."

"Daddy says you had a double lung transplant, and you might be confused. Because of morphine."

Morphine, yes, but not confused. Just not ready to tell a child that he was breathing with treasure from a dead man's chest.

Spreading the Chaos

Mark Newman

He is taking groceries into the house, an obedient little puppy; his wife directing him as if this is something that needs supervision.

Out the window she yells 'oi, shit brains. I've had the abortion, so screw you, have it all your way'.

He looks on with a bemused expression, a lost little boy, unsure which way to turn. His wife punches him on the shoulder; still he holds her gaze.

She winds the window up; gives a mock salute and drives away.

She has never seen this man before. This is just something she does; spreading the chaos.

Maturity

Jude Higgins

I'll avoid sitting on cold flag stones, swimming on a full stomach, going out with wet hair, bringing lilacs into the house or trusting men whose eyebrows meet in the middle.

I'll wear a dress – sometimes heels, attend my degree ceremonies, get a proper job, stay married, have babies, cook roast dinners, celebrate Christmas, visit relatives, hold family gatherings, stop causing arguments. Be kind.

I'll do what I want, even if my mother wants it too.

Even if it makes me happy.

Stiff

Joanna Campbell

When our Rose wouldn't put her arms in the sleeves of her best frock, Mam wept. Not just because of wanting Rose beautiful, but on account of the photographer charging by the minute.

"We're up to a week's housekeeping already," Mam hissed, pinching Rose's cheeks to raise a bloom.

I imagined four loaves, three quarts of milk and a string of prime sausage floating out the window.

Rose were right starchy-stiff. I couldn't twist her arm.

So I crouched behind and pushed my arms through her sleeves, lacing my fingers, just how our Mam wanted the corpse to look.

Author Information

We don't have enough room in a volume such as this to list a full biography for all of our authors, and anyway, we don't have to when they have all already done the job for us on their blogs and websites.

So, below, please find a list of the places on the World-Wide Web where you can follow up the authors from this anthology (where available). Please read their other work, buy their books, and generally support them. That way they can continue to bring you wonderful stories like the ones you've just read.

Alex Reece Abbott	www.alexreeceabbott.info
Amanda Quinn	@amandaqwriter
Amy Mackelden	clarissaexplainsfuckall.com
Angela Readman	@angelareadman
Angi Holden	@josephsyard
Anna Nazarova-Evans	@AnitchkaNE.
Barbara Leahy	@barbleahy
Bart Van Goethem	bartvangoethem.com
Beverly C. Lucey	beverlyc.lucey@gmail.com
Calum Kerr	calumkerr.co.uk
Cath Bore	cathbore.wordpress.com
Cathy Lennon	@clenpen
Chris Stanley	whenonlywordsareleft.wordpress.com
Diane Simmons	dianesimmons.wix.com/dianesimmons
Else Fitzgerald	noplaceelsewhere.blogspot.com
Emeline Morin	@EmelineMMimie
Emily Koch	emilykoch.co.uk
Garreth Wilcock	garrethwilcock.com
Gemma Govier	twitter.com/GGovier
H Anthony Hildebrand	@hahildebrand
Ian Shine	ianshinejournalism.blogspot.co.uk
Ingrid Jendrzejewski	www.ingridj.com
Vicky Newham	vickynewham.com
James Coates	@Brev_
James Norcliffe	jamesnorcliffe.com

Jamie Hubner	@Jhubs4
Jane Cooper	janecooperfiction.wordpress.com
Jane Roberts	janeehroberts.wordpress.com
Joanna Campbell	joanna-campbell.com
Jon Volkmer	jvolkmer.wix.com/jonvolkmerhomepage
Jonathan Pinnock	jonathanpinnock.com
Jude Higgins	judehiggins.com
Kate Mahony	facebook.com/KateMahonyWriter
Keith Gillison	thebosskillers.com
Kevlin Henney	semantic.net
Kirsten McKenzie	kirstenmckenzie.com
KM Elkes	kmelkes.co.uk
Laura Tansley	@laura_tans
Marie Gethins	@MarieGethins
Mark Newman	marknewman1973.wordpress.com
Michelle Elvy	michelleelvy.com
Mike Scott Thomson	mikescottthomson.com
Nick Triplow	nicktriplow.blogspot.co.uk
Nik Perring	nikperring.com
Nod Ghosh	nodghosh.com
Nuala Ní Chonchúir	nualanichonchuir.com
Pauline Masurel	unfurling.net
Richard Holt	bigstorysmall.com
Ruth Doris	@roodors
Sandra Kohls	@pinkpalinka
Santino Prinzi	tinoprinzi.wordpress.com
Sarah Hilary	@Sarah_Hilary
Shirley Golden	shirleygolden.net
SJI Holliday	sjiholliday.com
Sonya Oldwin	sonyca.wordpress.com.
Susan Carey	amsterdamoriole.wordpress.com
Susan Howe	howesue.wordpress.com
Tim Stevenson	timjstevenson@hp.com
Timothy Mark Roberts	timstermatic.com
Tracey Upchurch	traceyupchurch.com
Vanessa Savage	@VvSavage

Acknowledgements etc.

This year, perhaps more than any other, the putting together of National Flash-Fiction Day, and of this book in particular, has been a team effort.

First thanks must go to my co-editor, Angi, for her sterling work in helping me choose the stories in this collection.

Thanks also to all the writers who submitted stories to this anthology and made my and Angi's job so hard.

Congratulations to the winners of the Micro-Fiction competition who grace the final pages—and thanks to all those who entered as well as the judges: Angela Readman, Kevlin Henney, Cathy Bryant, Jon Pinnock, Cathy Lennon and Tim Stevenson.

Massive thanks need to go to Amy Mackelden and Tino Prinzi who run the engine room that keeps everything moving along. This book really would not have happened without them.

Thanks to Diane Simmons and Jane Roberts for proof-reading duties

In the wider NFFD-verse I'd also like to mention Tim (again) for doing such a good job of keeping the website up to date, and also the crew of the good ship *FlashFlood* (Susi, Shirley, Annette, Caroline, Sue, Cassandra) for all the work and support.

Finally, as ever, the thanks go to you, dear reader. We do this for you, we hope you enjoy it, and we appreciate you. We really do.

Calum Kerr
Director of NFFD

Also Available from
National Flash-Fiction Day

Jawbreakers
(NFFD 2012)
Includes stories from Ian Rankin, Vanessa Gebbie, Jenn Ashworth, Tania Hershman, David Gaffney, Trevor Byrne, Jen Campbell, Jonathan Pinnock, Calum Kerr, Valerie O'Riordan and many more.

Scraps
(NFFD 2013)
All of the stories in this collection have been inspired by other works of art: paintings, sculptures, TV programmes, films, music and more. As a result they are imbued with something of the original, but then take off into new and often surprising directions.

Eating My Words
(NFFD 2014)
Given the theme of 'The Senses' these writers have responded in unexpected ways to produce tales of love and betrayal, hope and despair, life and death. Writers include sci-fi and crime best-seller Michael Marshall Smith, crime novelist Sarah Hillary, Costa Short-Story Prize 2014 winner Angela Readman, NFFD Director Calum Kerr and a host of others including Nuala Ní Chonchúir, Nik Perring, Nigel McLoughlin, Cathy Bryant, Tim Stevenson, Tania Hershman and Jon Pinnock.

Other books from **Gumbo Press**:

www.gumbopress.co.uk

On Cleanliness and Other Stories

by Tim Stevenson

Thirteen stories that journey between the gothic past and the very far future: where a washing machine arrives unannounced to change the course of a life, and the colours at the end of the world are our oldest enemy. Discover why the mushrooms in the cellar bite back, how a little girl's birthday present can have a life of its own, and why, in the wrong hands, imaginary guns can still be very, very dangerous.

28 Far Cries by Marc Nash

This latest collection of flash-fictions from Marc Nash The stories range from the violence of Happy Hour to armoured pole-dancers, from dying superheroes to synesthesia, and from toxic relationships to warlords to the mythic ponderings of incubi and succubi. Each flash-fiction is crafted with Nash's usual close attention to detail and the nuances of language, to captivate and intrigue.

Rapture and what comes after

by Virginia Moffatt

For every tale of everlasting love... You'll find another full of heartbreak and misery Where other love stories end with the coming of the light, Virginia Moffatt goes beyond to show the darkness which can exist in even the happiest relationships. These stories are by turns funny, sad, heart-warming and heart-breaking.

The Book of Small Changes

by Tim Stevenson

This collection takes its inspiration from the Chinese I Ching: where the sea mourns for those it has lost, encyclopaedia sales-men weave their accidental magic, and the only true gift for a king is the silence of snow.

Enough by Valerie O'Riordan
Fake mermaids and conjoined twins, Johannes Gutenberg, airplane sex, anti-terrorism agricultural advice, Bluebeard and more. Ten flash-fictions.

Threshold by David Hartley
Threshold explores the surreal and the strange through thirteen flash-fictions which take us from a neighbour's garden, out into space, and even as far as Preston. But which Preston?

Undead at Heart by Calum Kerr
War of the Worlds meets *The Walking Dead* in this novel from Calum Kerr, author of *31* and *Braking Distance*

The World in a Flash: How to Write Flash-Fiction by Calum Kerr
A guide for beginners and experienced writers alike to give you insight into the world of flash-fiction. Chapters focus on a range of aspects, with exercises for you to try.

The 2014 Flash365 Collections
by Calum Kerr

Apocalypse
It's the end of the world as we know it. Fire is raining from the sky, monsters are rising from the deep., and the human race is caught in the middle.

The Audacious Adventuress
Our intrepid heroine, Lucy Burkhampton, is orphaned and swindled by her evil nemesis, Lord Diehardt. She must seek a way to prove her right to her family's wealth, to defeat her enemy, and more than anything, to stay alive.

The Grandmaster
Unrelated strangers are being murdered in a brutal fashion. Now it's up to crime-scene cleaner Mike Chambers, with the help of the police, to track down the killer and stop the trail of carnage.

Lunch Hour
One office. Many lives. It is that time of day: the time for poorly-filled, pre-packaged sandwiches; the time to run errands you won't have enough time for; the time to fall in love, to kill or be killed, to take advice from an alien. It's the Lunch Hour.

Time
Time. It's running out. It's flying. It's the most precious thing, and yet it never slows, never stops, never waits. In this collection we visit the past, the future, and sometimes a present we no longer recognise. And it's all about time.

In Conversation with Bob and Jim
Bob and Jim have been friends for forty years, but still have plenty to say to each other - usually accompanied by a libation or two. This collections shines a light on an enduring relationship, the ups and downs, and the prospect of oncoming mortality. It is funny and poignant, and entirely told in dialogue.

Saga
One Family. Seven Generations.
Spanning 1865 to 2014, *Saga* follows a single family as it grows and changes. Stories cover war and peace, birth and death, love and loss, are all set against a background of change More than anything, however, these are stories of people and of family.

Strange is the New Black
Spaceships and aliens, alternative histories and parallel universes, robots, computers, faraway worlds, run-away science and the end of the world; all these and more are the province of science-fiction, and all these and more can be found in this new collection.

The Ultimate Quest

Our heroine Lucy Burkhampton, swindled heiress and traveller through the worlds of literature, is now jumping from genre to genre in search of a mythical figure known only as The Author. Can she reach the real world? Can she escape the deadly clutches of her enemy? Can she finally reclaim her family name?

There's only one way to find out.

Read on...

Christmas

Jeff and Maddie are hosting Christmas this year, for their two boys - Ethan and Jake - for her parents, his father, his brother James and partner Gemma, and for a surprise guest. It's a time of peace and joy, but how long can that last when a family comes together?

Graduation Day

It's Graduation Day, a time for celebration, but for a group of students, their family and their friends, it is going to be a day of terror as the whole ceremony is taken hostage. In the audience sits the target of the terrorists' intentions: Senator Eleanor Thornton. But not far away from her is a man who might just make a difference: former-FBI Agent Jim Sikorski. Can he foil their plans and save the hostages, or will terror rule the day?

Post Apocalypse

Fire fell from the skies, the dead rose from the ground, and aliens watched from orbit as the Great Old Ones enslaved the human race. That was the Apocalypse. This is what happened next. Brandon returns, in thrall, and Todd continues his worship. Jackson finds unconventional ways to fight back, and General Xorle-Jian-Splein takes new control of his mission. The world has ended, but in these 31 flash-fictions, the story continues.

The 2014 Flash365 Anthology

12 Books 365 New Flash-Fictions All in one volume. This book contains: Apocalypse The Audacious Adventuress The Grandmaster Lunch Hour Time In Conversation with Bob and Jim Saga Strange is the New Black The Ultimate Quest Christmas Graduation Day Post Apocalypse 12 books full of tiny stories crossing and mixing genres: crime, science-fiction, horror, stream-of-consciousness, surrealism, comedy, romance, realism, adventure and more. From the end of the world to the start of a life; families being happy and families in trouble; travelling in time and staying in the moment, this volume brings you every kind of story told in every kind of way.